The Globbatrotter

Patricia Sumner

Illustrated by Dewin Blewog

All rights reserved, no part of this publication may be reproduced or transmitted by any means whatsoever without the prior permission of the publisher.

Text © Patricia Sumner
Illustrations © Dewin Blewog
Cover image © Dewin Blewog

Edited by Kelli Hill

ISBN: 978-1-916756-17-5
Ginger Fyre Press
March 2024

Ginger Fyre press is an imprint of Veneficia Publications
veneficiapublications.com/ginger-fyre-press

For Will who, as an infant, misread a logo on the side of a lorry and decided it would be the ideal name for a little creature with a piggy snout and piggy ears. The creature would also have a fondness for iced buns.

And for Ana who, as a youngster, lost her yellow rubber duck at a duck race party. It floated off down the stream to begin a new life – and she never, ever forgot about it.

In memory of
Patrick James Sumner
who loved the Somerset Levels

CONTENTS

PART 1

Chapter 1: The Hippy Wizard 1

Chapter 2: The Yurt 5

Chapter 3: Ghost House...................................... 10

Chapter 4: Yumdingoberry Jam 14

Chapter 5: Aunt Morgana................................... 19

Chapter 6: The Laboratory 24

Chapter 7: Tibetan Toadstools and Lamsinpoo . 29

Chapter 8: The Size of a Mouse 32

Chapter 9: The Globbatrotter 36

Chapter 10: The Tea & Biscuit 42

PART 2

Chapter 1: Jealousy 48

Chapter 2: Farewell To Norman......................... 52

Chapter 3: Stealing Worts 56

Chapter 4: The Sorceress 64

Chapter 5: The Fish House................................. 67

Chapter 6: The Midnight Meeting of Fur and Feather 72

Chapter 7: The Quest Begins 84

Chapter 8: The River Brue 90

Chapter 9: The Ambush 100

Chapter 10: Prisoners 110

PART 3

Chapter 1: Enough is Enough 122

Chapter 2: Stinky Cheese and Soggy Crackers 126

Chapter 3: Chomolungma 135

Chapter 4: The Sorceress Returns 138

Chapter 5: Impossible Journeys 150

Chapter 6: Icing Buns 157

Chapter 7: Sword-in-the-Stone 164

Chapter 8: The Most Precious Gift 177

Chapter 9: A Sparkling Teardrop 181

Chapter 10: Wookey Manor 190

Shakespearean References i
Acknowledgements v

PART I

CHAPTER 1: THE HIPPY WIZARD

Neptune had never had the nerve to tell his friends his real name. Unlike his father, he didn't think that being named after an ancient god of the sea was particularly cool – in fact, it was quite embarrassing. So, it had been a stroke of luck that on his first day at his new school, when the teacher had asked him his name, he'd said Nep very quietly. She thought he'd said Ned and, thankfully, that name had stuck ever since.

"That wasn't a goal! I wasn't ready," shouted Jesh.

"Of course, it was!" screamed Mary.

Neptune was used to his friends arguing about football.

"Ned, that wasn't a goal, was it?" said Jesh.

"Don't know," said Nep absently. He wasn't really concentrating on the game because he couldn't help glancing towards the backdoor of his house every once in a while. He was praying his father wouldn't emerge.

And then it happened. Neptune's dad stuck his yeti-like head around the backdoor.

"Hey, guys. Like, chill, dudes."

Nep cringed. He'd hoped Mary and Jesh wouldn't have to meet his father. It was always risky bringing friends home.

The children's mouths gaped like chicks waiting for food. Nep's dad just smiled and disappeared again.

"Ned, was… was that your dad?" Mary asked.

"'Fraid so."

"Wow," said Jesh, his eyes popping.

Nep was just about to say, *"I know, embarrassing, isn't it?"* when they chanted in unison, "Cool!"

Nep's dad was a one-off: an aging hippy with wild grey hair that billowed over his shoulders, and a bushy beard that looked more like a nest. He was also a scientist; he concocted medicines from herbs and rare plants which he collected from all over the world. He was an expert in his field, but the strange clothes he wore made him look more like a wizard than a scientist. People in the village avoided him; they thought he was either eccentric or mad.

"What does your dad do? Is he in a band?" asked Jesh.

They were intrigued; no one else in the school had a father like Nep's.

"He's a botanist and a herbalist," Nep replied.

"A what?" said Jesh.

"A plant scientist," Nep explained.

"Oh," said Jesh.

"He has a lab in the house."

"That's *well* cool."

2

Maybe hippy-wizard fathers weren't so bad after all. Jesh and Mary were mesmerised. They didn't seem to mind that Nep's dad was trapped in a sixties' time warp and wore tiny round glasses and knee-length robes. Jonathan York, the richest boy in the school, boasted that his dad drove a Porsche and listened to rap full blast. Nep's dad drove around in an ancient Morris Minor Estate called Aphrodite and listened to *Procol Harum*.

Mary, Jesh and Nep continued to play, though Nep's heart wasn't in it. Football wasn't really his game. He preferred tiddlywinks, origami and patience – anything he could play on his own, to keep himself entertained while his dad worked in his lab. Sometimes he'd help his father to mix potions or pour liquids into bottles, but he was never allowed to venture into the lab on his own.

"Goal!" screamed Mary.

"Offside!" bellowed Jesh, his face murderous.

"Oh, come on! Ned, wasn't that a goal?" said Mary.

"Didn't see."

Nep's dad popped his bushy head around the door again. "Peace, guys, peace! Spread the love, man."

"Uh... yes, Mr Trout... sure," said Jesh.

Mary just gawped.

"It's Bob, man," he smiled. "Just call me Bob."

"Okay... thanks, Bob," said Jesh.

"Hey, Neppy," Bob added, "have you been eating the iced buns?"

"No."

"Who's Neppy?" asked Mary.

"Oh, Dad just calls me that sometimes," Nep mumbled, blushing poppy red.

"They keep disappearing," Bob continued.

"I don't even like iced buns," Nep said.

"Must be the globster," sighed Bob, disappearing inside.

"The who?" said Mary.

Nep just shrugged. Sometimes even he didn't know what his father was on about.

CHAPTER 2: THE YURT

It was late in the afternoon and Nep's friends had gone home.

Nep slipped into the lab to find his father crushing some herbs with a mortar and pestle.

Bob looked up and smiled.

"I'm getting low on itchicara tree bark and lamsinpoo. I'm going to head off to the Himalayas soon."

"What do you need them for, Dad?" asked Nep.

"They're like good for humankind, dude. They ease people's pain and suffering."

Nep's father was on a mission to save the world. For the time being, he treated a few brave patients who came to the house to try out his remedies. They tended to be like-minded folk who believed in natural cures – and in *Procol Harum*. But they looked like a relaxed and happy lot, so maybe Bob's potions actually worked.

"I know that, Dad," said Nep, "but what do they *do*?"

"Well, the itchicara tree is a major miracle. Its bark cures rashes, its leaves cure sneezing, and its roots are the only known remedy for hiccups."

"Really?"

"Yeah, wild, isn't it?" beamed Bob.

"And the other plant?"

"Oh yeah, lamsinpoo. It's just mega, Nep. Fantastic for pain relief. And if you add it to any other herbal remedy, it makes its effect twice as strong."

"Really?"

"Oh yeah, it's the real deal."

"What's that one?" Nep asked, pointing at a bottle with an illegible label. It was the only pink liquid on a long shelf of slime-green and mud-brown potions.

"That's the juice of the famous Tibetan shrinking toadstool."

"The what?"

"The Tibetan shrinking toadstool, man."

"Never heard of it."

"It has *amazing* powers. If you have a spot or a wart, it'll halve its size in just a few minutes."

"That *is* amazing."

"But a word of warning," Bob said, peering over his John Lennon specs, suddenly serious, "don't ever mix it with lamsinpoo. I mean it, Nep, don't ever do that."

"Why not?"

"Legend says, it shrank the abominable snowman to the size of a ping-pong ball."

Nep laughed; his dad had a whacky sense of humour.

But, looking over his glasses again, Bob added, "Well, I mean, no one's seen the yeti in years, have they?"

That evening, Bob lit a fire by the tent at the bottom of the garden and put a pot of bean stew on the flames to warm. He liked living in the yurt in the summer months; he enjoyed sleeping under the stars. He said he felt closer to Mother Nature, closer to "like all this wonder, man", and Nep had to agree. Okay, the stew had been cooking in the kitchen oven for the last two hours, but Bob carried it to the campfire with great ceremony and, somehow, the food always tasted better for the few minutes it spent over the flames.

Bob dolloped the sizzling stew into his son's bowl and passed it to him.

"There you go, Neppy."

"Dad, why don't you call me Ned like everyone else?"

"Because your mother and I named you Neptune, son. That's your name."

"But why Neptune? Why not John or David or Peter? Nobody in the entire world is called Neptune!"

"Neptune was the Romans' god of the sea, so that's like awesome, dude. It's like, *wow*. And we all came from the sea originally. When we could only slip and slide, we slid out of the waves into the slippery ooze and we like evolved... Diving into the briny waves is like finding our roots. It's like going home. So, Neptune's a mega name, son. An awesome name for an awesome guy."

When they got chilly, they snuggled under the blankets in the yurt, where the wine-red velvet drapes kept out the cold. It was also reassuring to know that Bob would be there if Nep had his recurring nightmare – the one with a confusion of dark smoke and a hazy, frightened face. It had haunted Nep since he was tiny.

As far as Nep was concerned, theirs was the most beautiful, most precious, most special tent in the world. In it, Nep's dad was all his. There were no distractions, no research to be done, no plants to pick, no potions to stir. Nep could snuggle up to the fuzzy warmth of his dad's beard and they could talk for hours.

In the yurt, Bob would tell Nep about his mum. Gwen had died when Nep was only an infant.

Bob said she was the essence of beauty, both inside and out. She was everything that is lovely and light and warm and kind. When Nep asked him if they'd been happy together, he just sighed, "She was far out, Nep. Outta sight."

"Are you sure you didn't eat those iced buns?" asked Bob after a while.

"Dad, I hate iced buns."

"And I'm sure I had a jar of yumdingoberry jam."

"Don't know," Nep yawned, drifting off to sleep.

"Wait till I see old Globby."

CHAPTER 3: GHOST HOUSE

Just over the garden wall was an empty house. It had been deserted for as long as anyone could remember – probably forever – and it was slowly falling down. There were holes in the roof where birds flew in to make nests in the loft. Bats lived there too and on warm summer evenings they would hurtle through the darkness; Bob said they were sweeping up the last of the light with their busy wings. Stray cats had litters of kittens in old cupboards, and mice scurried around the overgrown garden with its cherub statue and moss-covered sundial.

There was a hole in the bottom of the garden wall and sometimes Nep would see a mouse creep through into their own garden to explore. It wouldn't stay for long, though, because Pythagoras, Nep's grumpy cat, with an evil glint in his amber eyes, would be waiting to pounce. Pythagoras was the meanest cat in the entire world. You could never stroke or cuddle him; he seemed to hate everyone. Despite Bob and Nep having rescued him from a cat shelter, the brown Burmese didn't seem grateful at all. Even Bob, who didn't believe that anyone could be wicked, only misguided, said, "That sure is one evil cat."

Nep called the next-door house 'Ghost House' and invented terrible stories of hauntings and murders to tell his friends. It was easier that way – otherwise, they'd all want to go there. But Ghost House was Nep's secret place. In his head, he could hear his dad saying, "Hey, property is theft, kiddo. Nothing should be owned, just borrowed or shared." But Ghost House felt like Nep's. It was where he went to think. He would climb up their plum tree and clamber over the high garden wall whenever he felt bored. Bob didn't mind him going there, as long as he stayed in the downstairs rooms because the floorboards upstairs were rotten. And he was allowed to wander through the overgrown garden as long as he didn't go to the pond at the far end. Nep wasn't sure why his father insisted on this – the pond didn't look deep enough to be dangerous, but he did as he was told. Bob agreed that Nep shouldn't take his friends to Ghost House; he said it would be "like disrespectful to Mother Nature. Not everyone loves nature as much as we do. Tread softly, Neppy. Tread softly and don't leave footprints". Nep sort of knew what he meant.

Talking of footprints, Nep had a strange memory from when he was very young: he'd found some unusual tracks in a patch of mud near the hole in the garden wall. He knew, even as a youngster, that they hadn't been made by birds, mice or cats. They were odd, almost like tiny shoes. When he pointed them out to his father, Bob said they must have been made by rabbits or stoats. Nep told him that rabbits and stoats didn't wear boots. Bob just laughed. Then he tried convincing Nep that a duckling must have left the tracks. But Nep knew every creature, both living and extinct, in his animal encyclopaedia and he knew that the tracks didn't belong to a duck. Nep was about to argue when his father wandered off back towards their house. Bob was shaking his head and chuckling, "Little fella's getting careless." Maybe the neighbours were right; maybe Dad was slightly mad.

Nep sat for a silent hour in Ghost House watching a stray cat feeding and washing her kittens in an open drawer of a musty cupboard. She didn't mind him being there; she knew he wasn't a threat. Nep wondered if Pythagoras was the father.

But eventually Nep went home and found his dad tinkering with the car's engine. Aphrodite didn't sound in the best of health.

"Need to head off soon, Nep. The Himalayas are calling. Need to walk on the wild side."

"Can I come with you, Dad? Please?"

"No, kiddo, you've got to work hard at school."

"But it's the summer holidays."

As usual, he wasn't listening.

"Study that botany, son. Plants are like... major miracles."

"But we don't do botany at school."

"And quantum physics too. Helps us to see God in nature. Brings us closer to like... the heart of things, man."

"Dad, I just do spellings and sums; it's so boring. Anyway, it's the holidays. *Please* let me come with you."

But Bob's mind was already in the high peaks of the Himalayan Mountains.

"Need to find itchicara and lamsinpoo. I might get a few more Tibetan toadstools too. And, you never know, one of these days, I might just find the Tibetan love flower. That's my greatest ambition, Nep. It's like my destiny, man."

"What is it?"

"Oh, it's legendary. Incredibly rare. Grows on the highest, most dangerous slopes in the Himalayas. They say its petals are translucent like tear drops and its leaves are the shape of perfect hearts. Symbolises the love of the world."

"What does it do, Dad?"

"Just one tiny, see-through petal can turn hatred to love. It has huge implications, son. It could put an end to violence, bloodshed, war…" Bob's eyes were dreamy and faraway.

"Wow."

"One day… one day… I might just find it." His voice was breaking with emotion.

"When are you going, Dad?"

"Soon, kiddo. Kathmandu's calling."

Nep wasn't too worried; "soon" could be anywhere between an hour and a year – his dad's concept of time was legendary.

The car spluttered and coughed as Bob revved her engine.

"Dad, Aphrodite will never make it to the Himalayas."

"Hey, dude, I just want her to get me to the airport."

CHAPTER 4: YUMDINGOBERRY JAM

"Dad, where are you going?"

It was early the next morning and Bob was hurtling around the house with a rucksack, grabbing maps and vials, tickets and socks.

"I told you, Nep. The Himalayas."

"What? Today?!"

"Alarm clock didn't ring... plane leaves Bristol in two hours... gotta go."

"But you can't just leave! What about me?!"

"There are plenty of flapjacks and some more iced buns in the tin. They'll get you through today. Only keep an eye on them; they seem to be dwindling."

"I don't even like iced buns! How long will you be?" Nep's voice was screechy and desperate.

Bob stopped in his tracks.

"Oh, didn't I say? Aunt Morgana's coming to stay."

"*Nooooo!*" screamed Nep, horrified. "Not Aunt Morgana!"

"She hasn't been to stay in years, Nep. And she's not that bad."

"*You* don't have to stay with her!"

"She'll look after you while I'm gone, kiddo."

"I'd do a better job of looking after myself. She can't hear a thing and she forgets all about me. Sometimes I think she actually wants me to starve to death."

"I know she can be a little scatty. Runs in the family–"

"Scatty? She's bonkers! And she's really mean."

"Hey, that's not kind, dude. She *is* my half-sister, you know."

"And she's rude to me."

"Look, she's an important lady. She's married to Sir Theo Somebody-or-other. They live in a mansion not too far away–"

"And we're *never* invited to go there, are we, Dad? She thinks we're not good enough for them, that's why."

"It's called Wookey Manor or something," said Bob distractedly. "It's like, *wow!* Anyway, your aunt was lovely when you were a baby. She used to look after you all the time. You and your mum had many happy times with her."

But Nep was deep in thought.

"I didn't know Aunt Morgana liked *Star Wars*," he said, confused. "Though she does remind me a bit of a Wookiee – especially all that moaning and groaning."

"No, Wookey as in the village of Wookey. It's a village near Wells. Listen, I've really gotta go, little guy. I'll only be gone for a month."

"A month! Dad, you can't do this!" Nep could feel tears burning at the back of his eyes. He wanted to scream; he wanted to beg.

"Sorry, gotta dash. I'll miss my plane."

Bob sprinted off towards Aphrodite in his flip-flops. His walking boots were still by the front door; so was his raincoat. Bob threw his rucksack into the car, leapt in after it and slammed the door.

"*Dad!*" hollered Nep, holding up his footwear and anorak.

The car door flew open again and Bob raced back towards his son.

"Thanks, kiddo. It's gonna be wet."

A quick kiss on Nep's head and Bob was charging off again. He hurled the boots and coat in the same direction as the rucksack and shut the car door.

Nep suddenly felt very small and very alone. Even Pythagoras, not known for his gentleness, came and sat beside him and allowed Nep to stroke his head.

Aphrodite's engine spluttered and choked into action. A cloud of fumes and soot exploded from her exhaust pipe and Pythagoras bolted for his life, leaving Nep to cough on the doorstep.

Without warning, the car door flew open once more and Bob tore towards his son. He looked frantic. He engulfed Nep in a huge, hairy hug, clinging on to him, and Nep had to gulp back his tears.

"I'm sorry. I've got to go. My work's like really important, man. I wouldn't go if I didn't have to. It's only four weeks, and Morgana will be here by midday." Then, grinning, he added, "If I find a new plant, a new species, I'm going to name it after you: the Wonder of Neptune."

Nep tried to smile. The world felt almost bearable again. Then Bob kissed him on his forehead, as if he loved him more than life itself, and scuttled back to the car. In a cloud of thick black smoke, he was gone.

Nep didn't know what to do. He was used to being on his own, sometimes for hours, but his dad was always working in the lab. It seemed different now that his father wasn't in the same house or even the same village. Soon, he wouldn't even be in the same country.

He went to the kitchen to get himself a flapjack. He hadn't had any breakfast. The pantry looked sad and empty. Nep noticed that the lid of the cake tin had been knocked off, so he peered inside. There were four flapjacks and two iced buns. When he looked more closely, he could see that one of the iced buns had been nibbled. There were tiny teeth marks in the icing and crumbs in the tin.

How could mice have opened the cake tin? Nep wondered.

He took a flapjack, closed the lid securely and headed for Ghost House. He tucked the flapjack into his pyjama pocket as he climbed the plum tree and scaled the high wall in his bare feet.

The knee-high grass sparkled with dew. It was cold and refreshing as he brushed through it. The abandoned garden was long and narrow. There was a patio near the derelict house, its concrete slabs cracked and full of weeds. A mossy sundial stood on a plinth nearby and stepping stones led across the meadow-like lawn. Apple mint and rosebay willowherb swayed in the breeze. Butterflies danced in the sunlight and bees busied themselves in the flowers. Halfway down the garden, on a patch of gravel covered in herb Robert and pineapple weed, a statue of a naked cherub with a podgy belly and dainty angel wings glistened in the morning light. It balanced on the toes of one foot, as if it was about to take off into the air. At the end of the garden was a huge willow tree. Its branches drooped down to half-cover a pond. Nep could see dragonflies and mayflies skimming over its surface and a happy garden gnome with a red hat fishing on the bank, but he knew he wasn't supposed to go any closer.

Watching the insects and eating his flapjack, Nep didn't know how long he'd sat near the cherub, but suddenly, with a sinking feeling, he remembered Aunt Morgana and realised he should get dressed. Heading back towards the garden wall, he stubbed his toe on something hard and yelped.

"Ow!" he squealed, hopping up and down.

Something scuttled off into the grass – a dark shadow vanishing from sight. Nep thought it must have been a rabbit or a kitten. Then, glancing down to see what had hurt his toe, he couldn't comprehend what he was looking at. There was his old, metal roller-skate. It was a bit of an antique; he used to strap it onto his shoes. It had completely disappeared a few weeks ago. On top of the roller-skate, fastened down with shoelaces, was their last jar of yumdingoberry jam.

How have these things got here? It doesn't make sense, thought Nep.

Tied to the front of the roller-skate, like a tow rope, was another leather shoelace. But who had done this? This was *Nep's* secret place!

Suddenly, he heard the purr of an expensive car on the road and a tooting horn. Oh no, it must be Aunt Morgana! He climbed onto the crates, which were stacked against the wall, clambered into the branches of the plum tree and was soon back in his own garden. He sprinted into the house, bolted up the stairs to his bedroom and slammed the door shut.

CHAPTER 5: AUNT MORGANA

Nep must have let Aunt Morgana knock on the front door for several minutes while he put on his T-shirt and jeans. Then slowly he descended the stairs to let her in. He could see her massive silhouette through the opaque glass. By this time, her knocking was angry and insistent.

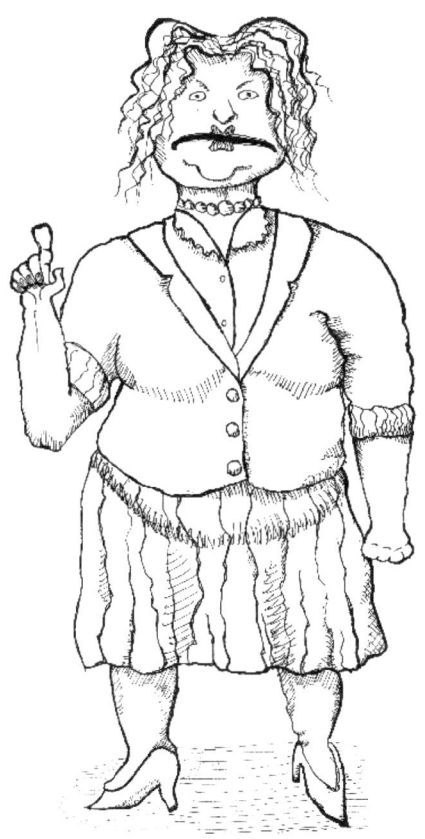

"Neptune! Neptune! Where are you?" she shouted.

"Neptune?" said her chauffeur, as he carried suitcases up the path.

Finally, Nep opened the door and was confronted by his aunt's red, scowling face.

"Where have you been, you impossible child? I've come all this way and you can't even let me in!" As she spoke, her double chin wobbled over her frilly collar and pearls, and her grey curls bounced on her head.

"Sorry, Aunt Morgana, I was getting dressed."

But she wasn't interested in excuses. She barged into the house as if she owned it, her ample frame knocking Nep sideways as she entered.

"I'll take my tea in the drawing room."

Nep wasn't quite sure if they had one of those.

"Driver," she called, without even glancing back, "you may return to Wookey and I'll call you when I require your services."

Her chauffeur staggered in with two heavy suitcases then two large hampers and dropped them in the hallway.

"Who's Neptune?" he asked, confused.

"God of the sea, I think," said Nep with a shrug.

Looking bewildered, the chauffeur returned to the Bentley.

No one ever came to the village of Meare in a Bentley. How was Neptune going to live this down?

Aunt Morgana had walked into the kitchen, back into the hallway and then into the sitting room. Now she was heading back towards the front door.

"Remind me, Neptune, where exactly is the drawing room?"

"Well, I draw in my bedroom sometimes..."

"Speak up, boy! Don't mumble. I can't stand it when people mumble."

Aunt Morgana bellowed like a charging hippo. In fact, she had many features that reminded Nep of a hippopotamus. She was large, round, had a huge face and neck, and as she was very deaf, she bellowed most of the time.

"Oh, this room will do," she sighed, going back into the sitting room.

She cleared books and scientific papers off the sofa and dropped them onto the floor with disdain.

"You really should have words with your maid. This simply isn't good enough. Sir Theodore Clarington-Smythe and I wouldn't tolerate such an appalling mess."

She flopped onto the sofa and put her feet up. Her flabby ankles sagged over her smart, heeled shoes.

"I'll take my tea now," she said.

Then, lying back, she closed her eyes and within thirty seconds was snoring like a pig.

So much for being looked after, thought Nep.

He'd had a flapjack for breakfast and there didn't seem to be any chance of lunch. Then he remembered the two large hampers. Aunt Morgana had arrived at their house in the past to find nothing in the pantry, even on Christmas Day, so she always came prepared with two *Harrods'* hampers. Nep didn't like the smoked salmon, olives and sherry, but the cartons of soup, packets of shortbread, and Dundee fruitcake were divine.

Nep unloaded the food and arranged it in the pantry and fridge. He was tempted to eat something there and then, but Aunt Morgana's temper was renowned. Then, with a huge effort, he dragged both of her suitcases up the stairs and put them in the guest room. Bob had remembered to put clean sheets in a pile on the chair, but he hadn't had time to make the bed. So, dutifully, Nep made the bed as best he could and tidied up the books, toys and journals that were lying around.

Now it was one o'clock and Nep was famished. He went down to the kitchen and made baked beans on toast for them both, using the last two slices of bread in the house. Feeling pleased with himself, he carried the tray into the sitting room where Aunt Morgana was just rousing.

"Good heavens above! What's that?!" she cried.

"Beans on toast."

"Do you mean people actually eat that?!" she said, aghast.

"It's all we've got."

"I know you live in a nasty, poky, little house and I live in a beautiful stately home, but this is beyond a joke."

"It's all we've got," Nep said again, trying to stay calm.

"Where are my hampers, Neptune? Where are they? I can't possibly eat this! And, good grief, look at your hands! They're filthy! When did you last wash?"

Nep looked at his hands. He had to admit, they were a bit grubby. In term-time, his father insisted on him showering each Sunday evening before the new school week. But this was the summer holidays and he couldn't remember when he'd last had a good wash.

"Two days ago," he said with as much conviction as he could muster.

Aunt Morgana shrieked.

"Right, no lunch for you until you've had a shower! And this is going in the bin. It's a health hazard! Sir Theodore Clarington-Smythe and I would never dream of eating anything as repulsive as this."

She marched off to the kitchen with the tray. Nep's dad would have ranted about starving families in the UK and abroad, and how we should never waste anything, but there was no point in arguing with Aunt Morgana Faye. No point at all.

"Go on!" she boomed. "Shower! Now!"

Nep's stomach rumbled loudly as he climbed the stairs to the bathroom. He'd just got undressed when he heard a knock on the front door.

Oh no, please don't let it be my friends.

Holding his breath, he opened the bathroom door just a crack to listen. To his horror, he heard Mary's voice.

"Is Ned there please?"

"Speak up, girl. Don't mumble," roared Aunt Morgana. "I can't stand it when people mumble."

"Is Ned there?" she said more loudly.

Nep could hear Jesh giggling in the background.

"Are you looking for Neptune Trout?" she bellowed.

They were both sniggering now. Nep bit his lip.

"He's in the shower. And he's not having any lunch until he's scrubbed his fingernails and washed behind his ears."

The giggling became uncontrollable. Nep put his head in his hands and groaned.

Aunt Morgana shut the front door and the two children went howling down the path. This was the end of everything. Nep was doomed.

CHAPTER 6: THE LABORATORY

Nep crept downstairs, his hair still dripping from the shower. He could hear clattering and banging. What was Aunt Morgana doing? She never did any housework.

Oh no, the noise was coming from the lab! No one was allowed in there. Then he heard the sound of smashing glass. Nep jumped down the last few steps and charged into the room.

Aunt Morgana was sweeping up two broken vials and dabbing at the floor with a yellow sponge. On the table in the centre of the room, where his father usually prepared and mixed herbs, she'd neatly laid out smoked salmon, olives and a glass of sherry. Everything else – his dad's precious experiments, drawings and notes – had been dumped in a pile on the floor. Nep was speechless. Who did she think she was?

"Sir Theodore Clarington-Smythe and I always dine in the dining room. When one is married to a baronet, one does have to maintain certain standards, you know. I refuse to eat beans on toast on a tray on my lap. It's demeaning."

Nep's speech returned in a furious torrent.

"I don't care who you're married to, you can't come in here! This is Dad's lab. No one's allowed in here without his permission."

"You mean this ramshackle, dusty room is some kind of laboratory?"

"Yes."

She burst out laughing. Her double chin wobbled like a jellyfish in a choppy sea.

"My father does very important work in here," Nep said, his blood boiling. "He can cure all sorts of illnesses. He's helping to ease humankind's pain."

At this, she put her hippopotamus head back and roared. And between each guffaw, she snorted loudly.

Nep was livid. Angry tears welled up in his eyes.

"You've got to put everything back where it was, right now!"

Aunt Morgana stopped laughing and glowered at him, her green eyes flashing with a hint of midnight blue.

"Oh, I've *got* to, have I? I think *you've* got to change your tone of voice, young man. You're extremely rude."

"No, you're the one who's rude. You've no right to be in here. You've moved everything round and broken things. This is Dad's work."

"Your father is nothing but a pathetic dropout," she said, grimacing with disgust. "A dirty, undisciplined hippy! I'm ashamed to be related to him."

Hot tears were trickling down Nep's face now.

"Don't you say that!"

"Oh, he pretends to be so clever and worldly and... and caring. But, mark my words, he'll come to nothing. He's a huge disappointment. And a terrible father."

"*Get out! Get out!*"

Nep was shaking all over. Even Aunt Morgana seemed to realise she'd gone too far.

"Now, I'll go and slice some crusty bread and when I return, I expect you to be calm, quiet and well-mannered."

She marched out of the room with her nose in the air.

Right! What can I do? Nep thought. *How can I end this nightmare?*

He tried to think quickly and carefully.

Dad's potions! There must be something on these shelves that will put Aunt Morgana out of action, at least for a while. If only Dad had found the famous Tibetan love flower; that would make Aunt Morgana change her ways!

He read along the lines of bottles: "Hungarian Wart Remover", "Yang Tin Hair Restorer". They wouldn't do any good. "Ugandan Mopo Seeds". He had no idea what they were. "Alaskan Blubber Creator – 4 drops to gain 1 extra stone in weight". Perish the thought! Then he saw something that might just do the trick: a small bottle of lime-green sludge. Its label read, "Kenyan Sleeping Potion – 1 small drop for a good night's sleep; 3 large drops to sleep for a week". With a quick calculation on his fingers, Nep worked out that twelve large drops would make Aunt Morgana sleep for a month. Then he wouldn't have to put up with her at all.

She was clanging about in the kitchen; he'd have to hurry. He unscrewed the lid and squeezed some of the liquid into the dropper. Carefully, he counted out twelve drops of bright green potion as they splashed into her glass of sherry. Then her footsteps were coming back down the hall. He screwed the lid back onto the bottle and put it on the shelf, just as she entered the room.

Aunt Morgana was carrying a small tray. Without saying a word, she put the sherry, olives and salmon onto it and turned to leave.

"I've decided you can stay in here until you've calmed down, Neptune. When you're ready to apologise, I'll let you out."

She barely glanced at him, though Nep thought her green eyes looked strangely dark. Then she took the key out of the lock, went into the hall and closed the door. Nep heard her put the tray down and then turn the key on the other side of the door. She picked up her food and went off to the kitchen.

He couldn't believe it. She'd locked him in! Nobody had ever locked Nep in anywhere. And he still hadn't had any lunch.

He looked around. There wasn't even a window in his father's lab. Bob had covered it over years ago to make extra space for shelves. Aunt Morgana was monumentally horrid.

But would she drink the sleeping potion? Nep put his ear to the door and listened. All was quiet. But after a few minutes, he heard her yawning loudly. She didn't seem to be able to stop.

"My goodness, that sherry was strong," he heard her say. Then there was more yawning. "Oh dear," she mumbled, staggering about. "Neptune," she called in a voice that was sleepy and slurred, "I'm going for a little nap. You can think about what you've done, you rude child."

Next, she was hauling herself, with some difficulty, up the stairs. But she didn't seem to make it to the bedroom. On the landing, there was a loud thud and a grunt. Shortly afterwards, he heard snoring that sounded like someone was moving furniture around on the floorboards upstairs. It was deafening.

Nep was amazed at how effective the potion had been.

Good old Dad! he thought.

He went back to the bottle of green potion to check what it said once more. When he turned the bottle round to look at the label on the back, it said: "For African Elephants Only".

Oh dear...

Now, how do I get out of here? pondered Nep.

He grabbed the door handle and shook it hard, but the door wouldn't open. He went to where the window used to be, but it was boarded up securely. In desperation, he decided to charge at the door. Screaming loudly, he ran at it full tilt, bashing into it with his shoulder.

"Ow!" he wailed.

Pain shot through his body, but the door hadn't budged. He rubbed his throbbing shoulder as realisation swept through him like frost. Aunt Morgana was going to be asleep for at least four weeks. Maybe four years! He was locked in the laboratory with no food, no water, nothing – nothing except jars of weird potions. His dad was probably miles away by now, flying on a plane above the clouds, and nobody knew where Nep was...

That was it, then. He was going to die.

CHAPTER 7: TIBETAN TOADSTOOLS AND LAMSINPOO

It wasn't working. Nep was levering at a tiny gap in the floorboards with a metal ruler. If he could just lift up two or three boards, he might be able to crawl out through the underfloor space. It wasn't likely, but it was worth a try. It was better than staying in the lab on his own. He struggled and strained until his face was crimson... Bang! The ruler snapped. What on earth was he going to do now?

He decided to shout. A neighbour or someone passing by might hear him and come to his rescue. Maybe Mary and Jesh were playing nearby. He took a deep breath and screamed as if he was being murdered.

"HELP! HELP ME! HELP!"

He meant it too – things were getting desperate. He shouted until his throat hurt. Then he went over to the door and listened. All he could hear was Aunt Morgana's monstrous snoring. Nobody would ever hear him over that racket. She was louder than a pneumatic drill. And, he remembered, the house was doubly insulated because Dad was trying to save the planet as well as humanity. It would be impossible to hear anything from outside.

Once again, Nep searched around the room for some means of escape. He could see light shining through a small crack in the bottom of the wooden door. The crack was about the height of an ice-lolly stick, but very narrow. He picked at it with his fingers to see if he could make it any bigger, but it was useless.

Like a lightning bolt, it came to him: *Tibetan shrinking toadstools and lamsinpoo!* But his father's warning was still ringing his ears: "I mean it, Nep, don't ever do that... It shrank the abominable snowman to the size of a ping-pong ball." But what choice did Nep have? He had to get out somehow.

He dashed across the room then stopped in his tracks. If the concoction actually worked, what would happen then? How small would he become? Small enough to get through that tiny crack in the door? And how long would it last? It was going to be a huge gamble.

Nep studied the lines of shelves. He knew the Tibetan shrinking toadstool was the pink liquid, with the illegible label, but where was the lamsinpoo? He read the bottles one by one. There it was, on the very highest shelf! He dragged a stool over to the bench and climbed up to reach it. The label said: "Essence of Lamsinpoo". The liquid was thick and black like treacle. His fate lay in these two repulsive-looking liquids.

Nep needed to work out how much to take. It was vitally important that he got it right. He didn't want to disappear altogether! Aunt Morgana's snores were shaking the house and making it difficult to concentrate. The label on the lamsinpoo bottle read: "2 drops twice a day to relieve pain". That wasn't much use. But his dad had said that if you added lamsinpoo to any other remedy, it would make its effect twice as strong. The label on the back of the Tibetan toadstools bottle said: "CAUTION! 1 drop 3 times a day to shrink boils and warts". So how much should he take? Nep was a lot bigger than a boil or a wart. His maths simply wasn't up to it.

Carefully, he squeezed out four drops of dark, sticky lamsinpoo into a test tube. Then he took the bottle of Tibetan toadstools and unscrewed the lid. Oh well, it probably wasn't going to work anyway. He was most likely going to die whether he took it or not. So, he didn't bother with the dropper; he just tipped in a good dollop of pink goo and the two liquids curdled into a gloopy sludge.

Oh boy...

This was it, the moment of truth. Nep shut his eyes and, trying not to retch at the bitter and revolting taste, knocked it back.

CHAPTER 8: THE SIZE OF A MOUSE

The world was blurry and spinning as Nep came to. His stomach gurgled and churned.

It must have knocked me out, he thought, feeling sick.

He sat up slowly, disorientated, and tried to focus. Little by little, the world began to clear and stand still.

"Oh... my... goodness."

The floorboard Nep was sitting on looked like a road. Its nails were manhole covers. The rows of jars and bottles on the shelves were the size of festival Portaloos. Feeling giddy, Nep looked up at the massive table leg, which resembled a giant redwood tree, towards the tabletop towering above him. It was just like looking up at a hill. And the ceiling beyond that? Well, it was as high as the sky, or space, or even outer space...

I must be the size of a mouse. This is what it must feel like to be a teeny-weeny mouse.

Nep suddenly remembered the crack in the door. Would he be small enough to squeeze through it?

Previously, it had taken him only a few steps to cross the lab – now it was quite a long walk. He hurried towards the door, realising that the crack in it no longer looked tiny; he was the same height as it!

I'm the size of an ice-lolly stick, he thought.

But the crack still looked very narrow. He turned sideways, breathed in and edged himself into it. Luckily, he took after his father. They were both skinny. In fact, Nep was scrawny. His dad said he had the legs of a seagull.

In he went. It was tight and he really didn't want to get stuck, but cautiously he eased his way through until he was out in the light on the other side of the door.

"Phew! Thank goodness for that!" he gasped.

Aunt Morgana's snores were even louder in the hallway; she was a human earthquake. Nep peered up the stairs to see her lying on the landing like a dozing walrus. The stairs were higher than Wells Cathedral! And the hallway to the kitchen looked like a motorway. But at least he was out of the laboratory. He'd done it; he was free.

His aunt was muttering something in her sleep. Then she began to laugh – though it wasn't her usual haughty-hippo laugh; it sounded more like an evil cackle.

"Arthur Pendragon... and gentle Guinevere..." she murmured sleepily. "When the names are in place, and the story retold..." Then she was mumbling again and snoring loudly.

She must be dreaming, thought Neptune.

He blinked and rubbed his eyes. A strange mist seemed to be hovering over her body – or was it just a shadow? He couldn't be sure because it was a long way off and his vision was still fuzzy.

He decided to make his way to the distant kitchen. He hoped he'd be able to find a drink or something to eat there.

Just as he reached the kitchen doorway, though, the hairs on the back of his neck stood up and he became frozen to the spot. He couldn't hear a thing over the noise of the rhythmic snoring upstairs, but he could feel a warm breeze behind him. A warm and slightly damp breeze. Gusts of breath were blowing onto his head and neck.

Slowly, very slowly, he turned his head to look over his shoulder.

"Aaaaaaaaghh!"

Pythagoras was crouching right behind him. He was bigger than the elephants at Bristol Zoo... Oh no! He was licking his lips.

Nep ran, but it was the worst thing he could have done. Pythagoras loved a chase and Nep's tiny legs didn't seem to be getting anywhere. Nep was about to turn round and shout at the massive brown cat, to see if he'd recognise him, when a huge paw knocked him flat on his chest. Nep was pinned down. He couldn't speak; he could barely breathe.

Don't eat me. Please don't eat me, prayed Nep.

Massive fangs sliced through his clothes, just missing his skin. Like great hooks, they whisked Nep up into the air and he dangled there like a caught mouse. Pythagoras trotted proudly through the kitchen, speeding up to a run. Nep couldn't even scream.

Oh no! The cat flap!

He braced himself and shut his eyes. CRASH!

"Ow!"

His whole face hurt. He'd hit the cat flap first, and at speed. His nose was bleeding and his face stung.

And then they were outside in the garden. Though he was flopping up and down like a limp puppet, Nep could just make out the patio flying past beneath him. Then giant dog daisies and tall grasses were whipping across his face. The herb garden flew by. They were fast approaching the end of the garden and the wall, but Pythagoras wasn't slowing down.

Not the plum tree! Oh please, not the tree.

Pythagoras leapt into the branches of the tree and scaled the trunk with his dagger-like claws. Up through the branches they climbed, up towards the sky. Nep was feeling sick and faint.

Then they were on the wall and lurching down onto the crates on the other side. And it was then that it dawned on him. They were going to Ghost House to see the stray cat. And Nep was going to be a meal for the new kittens. This was going to be his end. He really was going to die.

Suddenly, he heard a mighty roar beside him – a roar and then a ghastly squeal. Pythagoras dropped him and fled. And once again the world turned black as Nep passed out.

CHAPTER 9: THE GLOBBATROTTER

"Is you be feeling alright, small personage?" A deep growly voice was talking in Nep's ear – growly, but kind. "Is you able to be gettings up now? We can't be staying here. There be dangers."

Nep blinked as sunlight hit his eyes. His face was pounding and he felt weak.

"I don't feel very well," he managed to say.

"I don't supposes you does."

Then a handkerchief was dabbing at his nose.

"And I haven't eaten all day," added Nep sadly.

He tried hard to see. A blurry figure – broad, stocky, strong – was tramping off through the long grass. Nep heard muttering, panting, chopping. A few minutes later, a piece of plum the size of a watermelon was shoved into his hands. Nep dived into it, chewing and slurping hungrily. He'd never tasted anything so good in his life. Soon he started to feel a little stronger. He looked up and finally the world came into focus.

But what was it?

The creature's face was almost pig-like; its long snout sniffled and snuffled with a life of its own. Its skin was covered in orange hair. And on its head were two enormous floppy ears which stuck out horizontally on either side of its head. Nep wasn't sure if they were pig ears or donkey ears. But the creature couldn't be a pig or a donkey because it walked upright on two legs, and it was only slightly taller than Nep – who was still tiny. It wore big sturdy boots, a sheepskin waistcoat, and stripy drawstring trousers, a bit like pyjamas. The drawstring wasn't really needed, though, because the tummy the trousers tried to squeeze around was extremely large. Nep assumed the animal was a boy... well, a man... well, male.

"Be you a-staring at me?"

Nep couldn't reply.

"I's not liking to be stared at," he rumbled. "My kind be shy and private."

The creature's two little eyes were greatly magnified by thick glasses which were held in place by a fine, coiled spring that stretched around the back of his head.

"I be Merlin the Globbatrotter," he announced. "Merlin the Eighth, to be precise. Proud descendant of the first Merlin the Globbatrotter of the Isle of Avalon. And you be?"

"I be Neptune," croaked Nep. "I mean, I'm Neptune Trout, son of Bob. Pleased to meet you."

Bravely, Nep held out a shaky hand and the creature's sausage fingers shook it warmly. As the globbatrotter's bristles tickled his skin, Nep noticed that the animal had only three fingers and a thumb on each hand.

"Oh, I be hearing a lot about you," said the creature.

"Really?"

"Yeah. Only I be reckoning you to be somewhats bigger."

"I used to be. It's a long story... Was it you who saved me from Pythagoras?"

"Oh, I don't think there be any ancient Greek philosophisers in these parts," he said. "Norman be the only philosophiser I knows."

"No, Pythagoras is the name of my cat. That big cat that was carrying me."

"That be a strange name for a prickle-claw," said the globbatrotter.

"Dad called him that because he said he's 'all angles' – you know, teeth and claws?"

"No, I be not understanding..." said the creature, scratching his stubbly chin.

"Something to do with triangles?" said Nep vaguely.

"Nope... Anyways, I be charging that beast with my pokey-stick right up his flubble-bump."

"Oh, nasty... Well, thanks very much, I think you saved me."

"He be mean alright, that one. And there be plenty of them prickle-claws around here. We must be gettings out of sights."

With that, Merlin the Globbatrotter took Nep's hand and led him down Ghost House's long garden. Grass and knapweed towered above them like a jungle canopy, and they had to fight their way through. High above, two bees the size of Jack Russells droned loudly.

"Two bees, or not two bees, that be the question..."[1] muttered the globbatrotter quietly to himself.

"Pardon?" Nep said.

"Nothing, young'un. Just watch out for them pesky buzzers."

Nep followed closely behind the globbatrotter who clutched his 'pokey-stick' in his hand. It was a long spear carved from a twig and its point was extremely sharp. Over his shoulder, he carried a small bag with a buckle. Merlin was only a bit taller than Nep but he was a lot wider. If he'd been human, he would have been an Olympic shot-putter or a hammer-thrower. He looked immensely strong. Clumsy and awkward, he rolled from side to side on his stubby legs as he walked.

For what felt like an age, the two of them struggled through the grass to the bottom of the garden. As they approached the pond, which now looked like a great lake, the globbatrotter nodded and said, "Afternoon, Norman." But Nep couldn't see anyone. He wondered if another globbatrotter was hiding nearby in the undergrowth.

Merlin guided Nep round to the far side of the pond. Nep had never seen this part of the garden before; it had always been hidden by the trailing branches of the willow tree.

"Dad says I'm not supposed to come here," Nep said sheepishly, not wishing to offend his new friend.

"That be because I be living here."

"What? You mean Dad knows about you?"

"Oh yeah, he's the one who did be bringing me here longtimes ago."

"But why didn't he tell me about you?" asked Nep indignantly.

"I be a protected species, as you might say. Nobody but Bob is to be knowing about my whereabouts. I be his secret helper." Merlin the Globbatrotter looked deeply into Nep's eyes and said kindly, "He be going to tell you any-days now. You be old enough to be keeping secrets, methinks." He gave Nep a wink, his piggy eye blinking hugely behind its thick lens, then carried on walking. Over his shoulder, he added, "I be taking you to the Tea & Biscuit."

"Oh, I'd love some tea and biscuits," said Nep, still ravenous.

"No, *the* Tea & Biscuit – that be the name of my home."

As they entered the shade of the willow, Nep saw a big wooden tea tray floating on the pond and on it stood a huge silver teapot. Nep had seen teapots this size in the local community centre, but now, from his new and lowly perspective, it looked cottage-sized. Tied to a tall stick was a flag with the words "TEA AND BISCUIT. PRIVATE" and fastened to a mooring on the tray was a big rubber duck that bobbed jauntily on the water. Painted along her yellow side, in neat black letters, were the words "QUACKING NANCY". A jetty made of reeds and string led out from the bank to the tray.

"Careful you don't be slipping in there," said Merlin, nodding at the murky water.
"What's in there?" Nep asked nervously.

"Water, of course!" shrieked Merlin. His laughter was so loud it made Nep wince. Merlin's piggy squeals and snorts echoed across the pond.

Smoke was spiralling from the spout of the teapot, and a twig ladder led up to the teapot's lid, which was propped open, like a submarine hatch, on an old plastic knitting needle.

"Welcome aboard," Merlin chuckled proudly, allowing Nep to go before him. "You be the first human to ever be coming inside my humble home."

"Really?" Nep felt quite honoured.

"Well, you be the first human who be small enough!" snorted the globbatrotter. Then he was squealing again, his long ears flopping up and down as his huge head rocked back and forth.

Abruptly, he stopped laughing. He looked at Nep, his eyes watery and his voice trembling.

"Oh dear. I's been longing for some company. I haven't had a good laugh in multitudinous years. There only be me and Norman here, you sees. And, to be honest, he be quite serious. I's been feeling lonelysome. Neptune, I be very glad you came."

CHAPTER 10: THE TEA & BISCUIT

On the top floor of the Tea & Biscuit was a library with wooden shelves built around the circular walls. A single armchair stood in the centre of the room. Glancing at some of the books, Nep could see six volumes called *'History of Greek Philosophy'* by W. K. C. Guthrie; two volumes of *'Le Morte d'Arthur: The History of King Arthur and of his Noble Knights of the Round Table'* by Sir Thomas Malory; *'Wuthering Heights'* by Emily Brontë; and a huge, well-thumbed copy of *'The Complete Works of William Shakespeare'*.

"Wow, Mr Globbatrotter! You read difficult books!" said Nep, full of admiration.

"I be liking reading," he replied modestly. "And my name not be Mr Globbatrotter; it be Merlin *the* Globbatrotter." He sounded slightly offended. "A globbatrotter be what I am," he continued, "it be not my name. I be the last remaining globbatrotter in the whole widing world."

"Oh, I see. I'm sorry. No wonder you're lonely. What happened to all the others?"

The globbatrotter sighed deeply.

"It be a sad and terrifying story. I be telling you all about it laterwhiles."

Nep felt bad for asking.

"Which is your favourite book?" he asked, changing the subject.

"My particulars favourite be the works of the Bard hisself, Mr William Shakespeare. I be liking it when he says, 'We are such stuff as dreams are made on.'[2] I thinks that be very true," he said, nodding thoughtfully.

They climbed further down the ladder to the lower floor of the Tea & Biscuit and arrived in a cosy kitchen. A small stove burned cheerily beneath the teapot's spout. There was a table, two chairs and a dresser. The only light came from the stove's flickering flames, which made orange shadows dance around the tea-stained walls. Behind an old-fashioned screen was a hat stand, with a couple of items of clothes on it, and a beautiful four-poster bed. This is where Merlin slept.

"I like your home, Merlin the Globbatrotter. I like it a lot."

Merlin seemed relieved and pleased.

"I not be used to having visitors," he said coyly. "I hopes my manners be proper enough."

"So where does Norman sleep?" asked Nep, puzzled.

The globbatrotter chuckled, "Oh, Norman not be sleeping in here!"

"Oh, I see..." Nep said, but he didn't really see at all.

"These philosophisers, they be needing their own space to be a-thinking their great thoughts."

Merlin offered Nep a chair by the stove while he scurried about gathering food from the dresser for their supper. Hungrily, Nep ate big chunks of cheese and slices of juicy plum. Then afterwards, with great ceremony, Merlin brought out a large piece of iced bun. Nep didn't say anything, but suddenly everything started to fall into place.

"I be rather partial to icing buns," Merlin giggled, licking his lips with a huge pink tongue. "I be not able to resists them."

They sat beside each other, sipping camomile tea in front of the fire. By now, Nep was feeling much, much better.

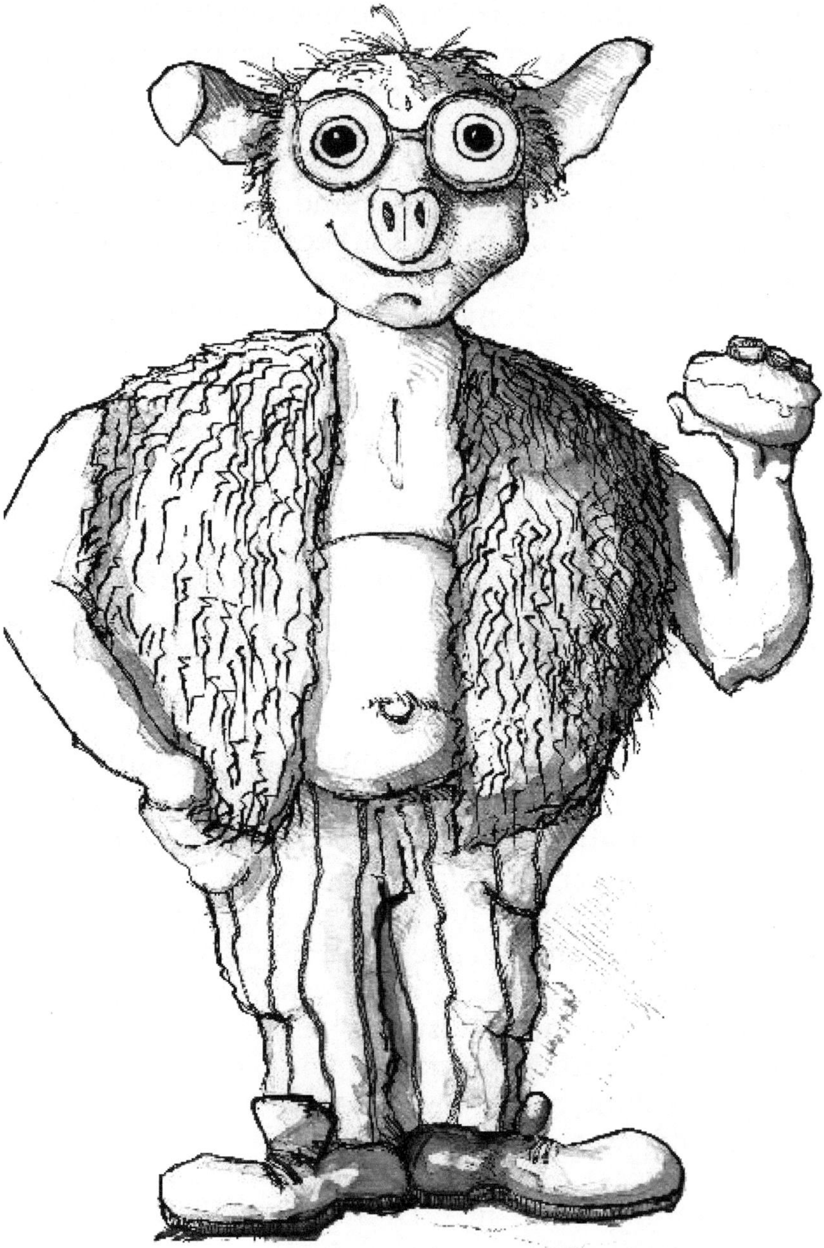

"Merlin the Globbatrotter..." he began.

"Yeah?"

"How did you manage to find all this furniture?"

"Oh, Mister Bob be helping me with that. He be getting Dolly's furniture for me, whoever she may be. The dresser, the table, the bed all be Dolly's furniture. I don't know what Dolly be thinking about it. Perhaps she can spare it."

"It's very nice," Nep said politely. "But what about the stove and all those books upstairs?" he asked. "They can't be from a doll's house... I mean, from Dolly's house."

"Well, Bob be clever with worts. I be teaching him over the years, you sees. He be dousing the books with Tibetan toadstools and lamsinpoo and they be shrinking. He be doing that with lots of things for me. We be a partnership, you sees. I be finding worts for he and helping he with magick spells, and he be giving me a home and looking after I. It be always like that with kings and globbatrotters."

Nep was quickly losing track of his meaning.

"Um... what does 'worts' mean?" he asked.

"Herbs, little'un. Nature's remedies. With my big hooter, I be sniffing out the roots and leaves for he."

"So, my dad sprinkled the potions onto these books? To make them shrink?"

"Yeah, he be sprinkling the books, the hat stand, the rugs and some of my clothes too. Bob gave me these jama-trousies. He be saying I not be decent walking around without them. Oh, Bob, he be funny!"

Nep sat up rigid, suddenly alarmed.

"But when will the potions wear off? When will all of these things get big again?"

"Oh no," snorted Merlin, "they not be wearing off. Otherwises my books be growing 'normous and breaking my teapot, you cabbage-head! It be a permanent effect."

"What?!" shrieked Nep, feeling hot and panicky. "But... but I took lamsinpoo and Tibetan shrinking toadstools to make myself this small."

"You be swallowing 'em?!" Merlin gasped.

"Yes," Nep said, turning pale.

"Oh, you's only supposed to be sprinkling the mixture, not swallowing it! You must be dickie in the noddle. You could be deadified."

Nep started to cry.

"I didn't know. I needed to escape. I had no choice."

"Now, now, don't be upsettifying yourself." The globbatrotter put a strong arm around Nep's shoulders. "There be an antidote, you knows."

"An antidote?"

"Yeah, a wort to be reversing the shrinking. A herb to be a-growing yourself again."

"Oh, thank goodness for that," sighed Nep, wiping his eyes.

"Now, let's be tucking you upways in your beddy-byes. You must be exhaustipated."

Merlin arranged a mattress and blankets on the floor for Nep in front of the stove. A chunky hand ruffled the boy's hair and within seconds, he was asleep.

"Oh dear, oh dear, what is we to be doing?" muttered the globbatrotter as he climbed into his bed. "Oh dear, oh dear. This be very bad."

PART 2

CHAPTER 1: JEALOUSY

"Cry havoc and let loose the clogs of war!"[3]

Nep woke with a start to a furious battle cry. With his heart pounding, he leapt from his makeshift bed, scuttled up the ladder, through the library, and up to the lid of the teapot. It was early morning and Merlin the Globbatrotter was standing on the tea tray, hurling clogs and boots at three enormous toads that were leering at him from the pond. They were as big and as terrifying as dinosaurs.

"Keeps back, little'un. Keeps back!" yelled Merlin. "Pass me my pokey-stick so I can rids us of these warty devils."

The spear was lying at the bottom of the twig ladder on the tray. Nep hurried down and handed it to Merlin.

"Will they hurt us?" Nep asked, his voice shaky.

"Oh no, they will not be hurting us; they will more likely be killing us!" Merlin waved anxiously at Nep. "Keeps back. They be the soldiers of the enemy – of the sorceress. Frogs be on our side; toads be on hers. This be bad, Neptune. Very bad. I haven't spotted toads in this 'ere garden for many a year. Evil must be returning."

Nep couldn't make sense of what the globbatrotter was saying, but he knew they were in danger. He saw a knitting needle near the Quacking Nancy and ran over to grab it. Being longer than a knight's lance, he could barely lift it.

Two of the toads watched Merlin and Nep from halfway across the pond, their gaze unblinking and malicious. But, to Nep's horror, the biggest and ugliest toad was swimming straight for the tray. Its cold eyes were a dark green, the colour of pond slime.

Summoning all his strength, Nep reached out and jabbed at the creature with the knitting needle. He prodded it sharply on the head, leaving a small dent. Reluctantly, the animal backed off.

"Brave Neptune! Brave warrior!" cheered Merlin. "You must be looking out for that Jealousy; he be a mean one alright."

"Jealousy?" Nep said.

Merlin pulled Nep away from the edge of the tray, back towards the teapot.

"Yeah, I knows this old devil," he said, pointing at the toad. "I calls him Jealousy because the Bard hisself do say that be the name of green-eyed monsters."[4]

49

The three amphibians had slid under the murky water and couldn't be seen. But Nep and Merlin knew they were approaching the Tea & Biscuit.

"What do we do?" asked Nep, trembling.

Two hideous heads appeared. Their unwebbed fingers grabbed onto the tea tray as they tried to heave themselves out of the water. The tray wobbled and tipped violently. Soon they'd all be in the water and, there, Nep and Merlin wouldn't stand a chance.

"Quick!" shouted Merlin. "We'll charge them on three. Five… four… three!"

They ran across the tray, screaming at the tops of their voices. Like jousting knights, they charged towards the ugly beasts.

"I'll thrippa thee!" yelled Merlin, prodding at them with his spear.

Reluctantly, two of the creatures dived down and swam for the edge of the pond. But where was Jealousy, the biggest toad? Suddenly, there was a massive thump under the corner of the tray as the toad tried to sink them with its powerful back.

"No, you don't!" shouted Merlin. He grabbed Nep's knitting needle and leapt onto the Quacking Nancy.

"Merlin!" Nep screamed. "Don't, it's too dangerous!"

The tray was rising and falling as the toad's blows sent shockwaves through it. Nep stumbled and nearly fell into the water. As the toad rammed the tray again, Nep grabbed the handle of the teapot and held on tight.

Merlin was magnificent. Using the knitting needle to stab down into the water, he drove the toad out from under the tray.

"I'll crack your noddle!" he roared.

"Be careful!" shouted Nep.

The Quacking Nancy was wobbling wildly.

"Go on, Jealousy!" roared the globbatrotter. "I knows you. Gets you going out of my pond!"

At last, the ungainly toad swam for the bank and crawled out of the water. Before leaving with the other toads, though, it turned to face Neptune and Merlin. Its eyes were furious and vengeful as it glowered at the globbatrotter. This appeared to be an old hatred, as old as time. But then its dark green eyes turned on Nep. They seemed to say, "*Make no mistake, I'll be back. And next time, I'll have you.*"

CHAPTER 2: FAREWELL TO NORMAN

Merlin the Globbatrotter, muttering that he had things to attend to, left Nep to finish his breakfast of football-sized raspberries and broken crackers in the Tea & Biscuit. As the globbatrotter struggled up the ladder to the teapot's lid, Neptune noticed that he was sniffing, sighing and rubbing his eyes. Feeling concerned for his friend, Nep followed him and poked his head out of the huge silver teapot. Despite the drizzle, he could see Merlin trudging towards the cheery garden gnome that stood on the far side of the pond.

"Friend, Norman, countryman, lend me your ears,"[5] began Merlin.

Leaning closer to the colourful gnome, the globbatrotter put a hefty arm around his clay shoulders and spoke into one of his chipped ears.

"Well, my mostings dear and learned friend," he said, "it would seem the time has come to be leaving you." He held up his chubby hand adamantly. "No, no, no, please be a-sparing me your words. They will be making me cry alls the more. I know you have your philosophising to do and you cannot be uprooting and accompanying I, but we have been friends for many a year outs and ins, and I be regarding you mostings highly."

At this point, Merlin sighed again, took a handkerchief out of his pocket and blew his snout loudly.

"No, no, you must be lettings I finish," he continued, raising a finger. "I knows you be a-feeling the sames way, for I can see it in your glinting twinkle-eye."

Just then, a raindrop trickled down the shiny cheek of the garden gnome.

"So, this must be the end of our friendlyship. You see, I promised Arthur that I would protect his young'un if ever that evil sorceress did return. I must venture with young Neptune into the waterways of Avalon to hide him from her devilish ways. I be only a humble fellow, but I have a duty to be keeping that small personage safe."

"But I can't leave!" called a voice from the top of the teapot.

Merlin turned to see Neptune hurrying down the ladder and jumping onto the tray.

"This is my home," cried Nep. "I live in the house next door. My aunt is unconscious on the landing. My dad's gone to the Himalayas for a month. Nobody knows where I am. And I'm the size of an ice lolly!" His voice was starting to crack.

"You cannot be staying here, you cabbage-head!" said the globbatrotter, trotting over to Neptune. "Any times now, Jealousy will be back with Morgan le Fay and all her evil powers and toady followers. They'll be rippin' out your tripes and trullibubs before you knows it. It be not safe, Neptune."

Nep didn't like the sound of that, but he simply couldn't leave.

"But nobody knows where I am," he cried. "How will my dad ever find me again?"

"You must be trusting I, young sir. I will be hiding you in the watery channels and rhynes, just as Bob instructed me. I cannot be letting them attackle you. Your father would never be forgiving me if I did not do my duty. And in a month, I will be sneaking you back to your home, all safies and soundies."

Neptune tried to calm his tiny, pounding heart.

"You mean Dad told you to hide me?"

"Indeedy he did, if ever this darkest of threats did occur. So, is my plan to your likings, Neptune?" asked the globbatrotter, his magnified eyes earnest and troubled.

"Okay then," said Nep, not feeling he really had a choice. "But I must return in a month, and somehow I must get back to my normal size."

"Indeedy so," said the globbatrotter. "As I be saying, I have a plan. I knows very well the subject of worts and potions – and spells too. I be not descended from Merlin the First for nothing, you knows. Now, we must be readying ourselves. We must be launching the Quacking Nancy into the channels of Avalon."

"Do you mean the Somerset Levels, Merlin? Are we going to paddle along the rhynes? Won't we get lost? Won't we drown?" Nep felt anxious and confused; the globbatrotter was making even less sense than Bob usually did. Could this strange creature be trusted at all?

"Yeah, Neptune. You and I will be returnings to my home of yore." The globbatrotter had a faraway look in his eyes. "But first I must be a-gathering my allies in the old Fish House. There's a Midnight Meeting of Fur and Feather to be had."

Nep wondered if the old globbatrotter was delusional or simply mad.

As Merlin guided Nep back to the Tea & Biscuit, the globbatrotter looked wistfully over his shoulder at the garden gnome with the bright red hat and cheery smile.

"I only hopes my friend the philosophiser will be safe. Goodbye, Norman, my quiet and pondering friend. I will not be forgetting you."

★

That night, as Nep tried to fall asleep on the mattress by the stove, Merlin the Globbatrotter was bustling about, gathering this and that to put in his shoulder bag – pieces of cheese, broken crackers, parchment, candles, matches, a small bottle of something, and a change of socks.

Nep tossed and turned as the clumsy creature bumped into furniture and muttered under his breath. Finally, the globbatrotter climbed into his four-poster bed.

Peace at last, thought Nep.

But then he could hear Merlin whispering to himself.

"In the middle of the night, when midnight starts to spark... no, when *magick* starts to spark. That's it. Animals of fur and feather... no, that's not right... um... how did it go? *Creatures* of fur and feather. That's right. Creatures of fur and feather shall have a get-together after dark. No, that's not right either."

Eventually the muttering turned to snoring and Nep could finally get some sleep.

CHAPTER 3: STEALING WORTS

Nep woke from a feverish dream – the dream he always dreaded having. The one he'd had since he was tiny, where he watched swirling mist creep around the face of a beautiful woman with a shining complexion. Frightened tears rolled down her cheeks. Her hand reached out desperately towards him. She was terrified and in danger, but there was nothing Nep could do to help. Slowly, she slipped away from sight.

As Nep opened his eyes, a huge face closely resembling a Tamworth pig was leaning over him, its snout almost touching his nose.

"Morning, Neptune," it said.

Nep jumped out of his skin.

"Oh, Merlin! It's you! What's the matter?"

Merlin looked worried.

"I do not be having everything I needs. I have mostings things prepared, but not all. There is some things that be missing."

"What do you mean?" asked the half-awake boy.

"There is certain worts I do be needing for my potions and spells. Certain worts that is contained in your father's labora-oratory."

"What?" said Nep, rubbing his eyes. "Oh, hang on. No! There's *no way* I'm going back into that house. Do you know how difficult it was to escape last time? And have you forgotten? Pythagoras tried to kill me!"

"I will be a-coming with you, Neptune. I will be protecting you with my pokey-stick. I be not able to be arranging my meeting tonight if I do not be having that deadly nightshade mixture, and this

Meeting of Fur and Feather be mostings crucial for your safety."

"Look, Merlin," snapped Nep, finally losing patience. "I have no idea what you're talking about most of the time. For someone who reads loads of clever books, you don't make much sense, do you?"

Immediately Merlin looked hurt; his little round eyes blinked sadly behind his thick spectacles.

"Sorry, Merlin," said Nep, hanging his head in shame. "Sorry. I'm just worried, that's all. I don't know what's going on... I want my dad. I miss him. And I don't want to be tiny anymore. I just want to go back to how things were – even if that means living with horrid Aunt Morgana for a month."

"What's that name you say?" asked the globbatrotter, suddenly suspicious.

"Aunt Morgana Faye," said Nep. "She's dead posh. She lives in a manor house somewhere. She's married to a clarinet or something."

"Ah, I thought it might be her," said Merlin, more to himself than to Nep. "Your father's half-sister, I supposes."

"Yes. Why? What's wrong?" asked Nep.

"Her name. It be too close for comfort, you sees. It be almost the same as the sorceress herself – Morgan le Fay."

"The sorceress with all the toads?" asked Nep.

"Yeah, her."

"What *is* a sorceress anyway?" asked Nep.

"You know, an evil human what does devilish magick."

"A witch?"

"No, no, no," said the globbatrotter, shaking his head. "Witches be kind and good. They pick worts and do be making healing potions; they treat nature with mostings respect and try to cure illness and sorrow."

"That sounds a bit like Dad," said Nep.

"It do indeed, do it not? But a sorceress be a cruel creature of darkness what enjoys inflicting pain and what wants nothing more than all-powerfulness for herself."

"Well, Aunt Morgana isn't a sorceress. I mean, she *can* be quite mean – even nasty at times, but she's just… she's just… I don't know what she is. But she's not a sorceress."

"I be sure you is right, young sir. But I still be a-needing that deadly nightshade."

"Isn't that poisonous, Merlin?"

"Oh yeah… mostings definitely. But I will not be a-swallowing it, you cabbage-head."

★

After hours of planning, instruction and practice, Nep couldn't believe he was making the long trek back to his house with his strange new friend, Merlin. The globbatrotter had a rope slung over his shoulder with a metal claw tied to the end of it, and between them, they carried a long knitting needle, which made the journey all the harder. By the time they reached the hole in the garden wall, Nep was worn out.

"Do we really need to go back to the house?" said Nep. "I mean, there must be some deadly nightshade growing round here somewhere. Couldn't we just pick some?"

"The deadly nightshade in the labora-oratory be already prepared by your dear father, you sees. It be mixed with dog violet and bird's-eye speedwell.

It be exactly what I do be needing to summon the creatures for a Meeting of Fur and Feather. There has not been a meeting of this kind for many a year outs and ins, and frankly, Neptune, I be not properly prepared for this sudden happenstance."

"Okay," sighed Nep. "Let's get it over with."

Just as they were about to drag the knitting needle through the hole in the garden wall, Nep had a flashback.

"It was you!" he cried.

"It were?" replied the globbatrotter, puzzled.

"The footprints in the mud, when I was little."

"You be rather little now, if you don't minds I saying."

"I *knew* they weren't made by a mouse or a rabbit or a duck. They were your boot prints!"

"Ah, maybe so," said Merlin, blushing. "Perhaps you did discover I."

"And my roller-skate!" added Nep, suddenly realising the truth. "You stole my roller-skate – and a jar of yumdingoberry jam!"

"Now, *excuses I...*" began Merlin indignantly.

But, just then, there was a loud rustling and two big eyes appeared in the jungle of grass behind them.

"It be one of them young prickle-claws," whispered Merlin. "More curious than dangerous at this age, but best we be hurrying along. His mother will not be far behind he."

They both dashed through the hole in the wall and into Nep's garden, which now looked vast. Glancing around anxiously, they checked that Pythagoras wasn't in sight, then they scuttled towards the cat flap in the backdoor, still carrying the plastic knitting needle.

"What be that?" asked Merlin as they approached the cat flap.

The flap was rising and falling gently, as if it was a gusty day, but there was no wind at all. Each time it lifted, a sound like growling reached them.

"That's Aunt Morgana," said Nep, raising his eyebrows.

"She be a human?" asked the globbatrotter warily.

"Oh yes, she be a snoring human," said Nep.

Merlin's eyes widened in disbelief. Then he heaved the knitting needle upwards until it was propping open the cat flap.

"In you go, young'un," he said to Nep. "And take this." Out of his bag, he took a small wooden pot with a lid. "We do not be needing much. Half a pot will do."

"Aren't you coming with me?" asked Nep, putting the wooden pot in his pocket.

"I will be keeping a-watch here and making sure this swinging door do not be swinging shut on you. Take this too," he said, passing Nep the long rope with the grappling hook.

"What if Pythagoras is inside the house?" whispered Nep.

Merlin just shrugged.

"Run?"

★

Once again, Nep was creeping down the motorway-sized hall. He couldn't hear anything over Aunt Morgana's terrible snoring; every time she breathed out, all the pictures on the walls rattled. He kept close to the skirting board, his eyes searching in every direction for their evil Burmese cat. Luckily, Pythagoras didn't seem to be at home.

When he reached his father's lab, Nep compared his own height with the crack in the door to assure himself that he could still fit through. He pushed the bundle of rope into the room and squeezed in after it.

Well, here I am again, thought Nep.

But he felt dizzy at the thought of trying to reach the potions on those towering shelves. Even with the long rope, it would be like climbing a high cliff. If he fell, that would be the end of him.

That's when Nep spotted a green spider plant above him, its straggly stems trailing almost to the floor. Each long stem had a small plantlet at the end of it. Perhaps he could climb up one of those to reach the wooden worktop? But the stems were very slippery. Each time he tried to clamber up, he slid back down to the floor.

So, he decided to use the rope with the grappling hook. Clutching the end of the rope in one hand, he started to swing the sharp claw back and forth, just as Merlin had taught him. When it was swinging well, with one motion, he released the coils of rope and flung the hook up towards the top of the wooden stool. Somehow, the hook clung fast.

Taking a deep breath, Nep slowly but surely climbed up the rope, gripping tightly with his hands, knees and ankles. He took it cautiously, but after a few minutes, he was standing on top of the stool – though it felt like he was standing on a high hill.

The next step was to pull the metal claw out of the wood, wind up the rope again, then throw it up to the work surface. This was much closer and easier, and soon Nep was standing on the worktop, peering around the enormous room.

"Deadly nightshade," he said to himself, "where are you?"

Before embarking on a daring and dangerous climb up the rickety shelves, he tried to read the labels on the jars high above him. He could make out some of the names, but the rest were just too far away. It would take him hours and hours to climb up there and work his way along every shelf – and he might never find the potion anyway. How he wished his father was more organised and put everything in alphabetical order, then he might stand a chance of finding the right jar.

It looks like Merlin won't be having his "mostings crucial" meeting after all, thought Nep.

He couldn't see the words 'Deadly Nightshade' anywhere, and he was just about to give up, when further along the worktop where he was standing, he spotted something: a small green jar with a label that said, 'Fur and Feather Potion'. It had been staring him in the face all along.

"That's it!" said Nep triumphantly. "Fur and Feather!"

When he reached the jar, which came up to his chest, he wondered how he was going to unscrew the lid. Luckily, his father hadn't fixed it on tightly, because when Nep pressed his two hands against it and pushed as hard as he could, it started to move. He kept leaning his weight against it and running round and round the jar until eventually the lid came loose. Feeling rather dizzy, Nep shoved the lid aside and leaned over the edge of the jar to reach inside with his wooden pot.

Whatever you do, don't fall in, he told himself, holding his breath. He knew the potion was poisonous if swallowed.

Taking great care not to get any of the mixture on his skin, he scooped up a potful of the thick brown contents – it had the consistency of soft, oily fudge. Then he replaced the wooden lid and put the little pot back in his pocket.

Next, he rubbed his hands in some old candle wax, which lay on a dusty saucer on the workbench. This made his skin feel smooth and slippery – a perfect lubricant to allow him to slide down the rope.

"Weeeeeeeee!" he cried as he whizzed, in a flash, down to the stool below.

But when he got there, his heart sank. It dawned on him, for the first time, that this part of the mission hadn't been planned or rehearsed. There was no way he could remove the grappling hook from the worktop above him, and it would be impossible to climb down the stool to the ground below. What was he going to do?

But then an even worse situation began to unfold: thick dark smoke was curling under the laboratory door.

CHAPTER 4: THE SORCERESS

Nep's mouth was dry and his heart was thumping. Where was the smoke coming from? Was the house on fire?

Plumes of grey mist were drifting under the door and rising into the lab. But that wasn't all; Aunt Morgana had started to laugh evilly again. Had the Kenyan sleeping potion driven her mad?

Then Nep heard those words; the ones his aunt had muttered nonsensically before. But this time his aunt's voice was clear and booming – in fact, it was terrifying. It didn't sound like Aunt Morgana at all.

> "When Arthur Pendragon
> and gentle Guinevere
> raise a babe to a child,
> then Morgan will appear.
> When the names are in place
> and the story retold,
> my power will return –
> dark sorcery of old."

The chilling verse was followed by more monstrous laughter, and all the time the cloud of smoke was growing thicker and thicker.

Nep yelped as the door started to rattle and bang as if something huge and alien was trying to break in.

And that was quite enough! He wasn't going to hang around any longer. But the only way out of the lab was through that crack in the bottom of the door – the door that was now smothered in swirling darkness.

Noticing a yellow sponge lying on the floor, where Aunt Morgana had tried to mop up his father's potions, without a second thought, Nep leapt off the stool, plummeted through the air and landed on his back. Thankfully, the sponge was thick enough to act as a trampoline and he bounced a couple of times before scrambling off and sprinting across the room. He pulled his T-shirt up over his mouth and nose because the smoke was acrid and vile; it smelt as if some poor animal had died.

With his arms reaching in front of him, he felt for the crack in the door and squeezed through. But out in the hallway, the smoke was even denser. He couldn't see a thing. For all he knew, Pythagoras, or even Aunt Morgana, could be crouching there, waiting to pounce.

He ran blindly through the billowing smog towards the backdoor and the cat flap.

"Run, Neptune!" came Merlin's urgent voice from down the hall. "It be she, Morgan le Fay!"

Panic-stricken, Nep raced towards his friend's distant cry.

As he neared the kitchen, the smog started to clear a little and he turned back to peer up the stairs. Aunt Morgana's body still lay on the landing, but tentacles of dark mist flowed from her mouth every time she exhaled. Somehow, the smoke was coming from inside her!

Nep froze in terror. He knew instinctively that whatever was causing the smoke was evil, cruel and not of this world.

Without warning, Aunt Morgana bent at the waist and sat upright like a stiff mannequin. She looked expressionless, inhuman. Darkness continued to billow from her mouth, but now it was streaming from her hollow eyes too.

"Aaaaaaaghhh!" screamed Nep, horrified.

"Run to me!" shouted the globbatrotter. "Run!"

But Nep couldn't take a single step.

His aunt's head was contorting repulsively. Her skin bulged out like a balloon on one side of her face and then on the other, as blue-grey mist flooded from her swollen skull.

Nep was whimpering now, unable to think or act or breathe.

But, in one rapid *whoosh*, the smoke that had trailed down the stairs was suddenly sucked backwards, to hang in the air above Aunt Morgana's body. Snake-like, it spiralled round and round until it formed the dark outline of a human form. The silhouette looked like a tall, slender woman in a flowing gown. Then, just as two holes appeared like pale eyes in the shadows, a hand grabbed Nep and hauled him towards the backdoor. It was Merlin the Globbatrotter.

"Come on, young sir," said Merlin. "I be seeing better-looking faces on pirate flags."

The two of them hurtled through the kitchen and dived out of the cat flap, glad to be engulfed in fresh air, blue sky and birdsong once more.

"Did you be getting it?" asked the globbatrotter, breathing hard, as he pulled Nep back through the hole in the garden wall towards Ghost House. "Did you be getting the potion?"

But Nep was still whining and moaning like an injured puppy. It would be a long time before calm and reason returned.

CHAPTER 5: THE FISH HOUSE

Instead of making their way back to the Tea & Biscuit, Merlin half-dragged, half-carried Nep in the opposite direction. With his glasses steamed up from his exertion, at first Merlin had thought that the garden behind Ghost House was moving; it looked to him as if a great wave was rolling across the grass. But then he realised that the ground was covered in a writhing mass of toads, all crawling towards the pond.

"This way," whispered Merlin to Nep. "Post-haste!"

He and the tiny boy dashed up the concrete path beside Ghost House's mouldy green wall. The path led them to a smaller garden at the front, which was just as unkempt as the back. The garden gate was rusty and hanging from one hinge, so it was easy to crawl underneath it. Then they hurried out onto the tarmac road. In the past, the road had always looked like a narrow lane to Nep, but now it was huge and frightening.

"Too dangerous," panted Nep – the first words he'd uttered in half an hour.

"Do not be afeared, young sir," said the globbatrotter with sweat dripping off his snout. "We will be keeping to the verge and no one will be seeing us. We must make for the Fish House. Morgan le Fay will not be finding us there, I can assure you. We must be a-gathering the creatures of the marshes. We needs their help more than I cares to say."

Nep shrieked and clutched onto a high stone wall as a car sped by. The noise and wind from its massive tyres were too much for his nerves to bear, especially after his recent ordeal.

"Courage, small personage," said Merlin, peeling Nep's fingers from the wall. "Come on now. We must be hurrying."

At the edge of the village stood a building constructed of stone, with tiny square windows and a small wooden door. It was known as the Abbot's Fish House because in medieval times it had acted as a fish store for the monks of Glastonbury Abbey. The fish had been caught from a nearby lake called Meare Pool, which had long since vanished. But some of the magic of Glastonbury still clung to the old Fish House's walls, and the animals of the area knew they could shelter there in times of danger or during harsh winters. A hole in the back wall gave little creatures access, and a crack in the tiled roof allowed birds and bats to sweep in. It was a secret place, full of memories and enchantments – a place where humans no longer set foot.

By the time Merlin and Nep reached the ancient building, the rosy light of evening was fading. They tumbled through the hole in the back wall and fell into the silence of the musty space. Feeling a little safer, Nep burst into tears.

"There, there, Neptune," said Merlin, putting a comforting hand on his thin arm. "What you saw was mostings terrible. Mostings distressing for a small human bean. Not many have witnessed Morgan le Fay in all her wickedness."

Nep could do nothing but weep. He was exhausted as much as he was frightened, and he was frightened as much as he was confused.

"Rest now. You be wearysome," said Merlin, taking off his woolly waistcoat to make a pillow for Nep. "I have some preparations to be a-making. Did you be discovering the potion in the labora-ora-oratory?"

Neptune passed the little wooden pot to the globbatrotter. "I had to leave the rope behind," he sniffed.

"Never you mind that now," said Merlin gently.

Then, crying softly to himself, Nep flopped down on the earthen floor to rest his tired head and aching limbs.

Into each corner of the large room, Merlin tipped some of the deadly nightshade, dog violet and bird's-eye speedwell potion.

"This will be keeping us safe from all evils while we be a-holding the Midnight Meeting of Fur and Feather. Be not afeared, young sir. There be no sorcery about to take place inside these 'ere walls, only *creature magick*. The good kind. The kind of magick what means always well."

Nep tried to nod in reply but he was utterly spent.

"And don't you be a-fretting when they arrive, now," said Merlin.

"When who arrives?" asked Nep sleepily.

"You will be seeing soon enough. They all be friends. They all be friends."

Then, as Nep closed his eyes, Merlin seemed to be scribbling on a piece of parchment. He was using the scratchiest, most annoying pen in the world – in fact, Nep thought it might be an old-fashioned quill.

"Kat-man-doooo. Um... that don't look right," said Merlin to himself. "Him-a-lay-azzz. That don't look right either. Now, how do you spell Pendragon?"

Finally, the globbatrotter folded up the piece of paper, put it in his bag and the building fell silent.

★

Meanwhile, at Nep's house, an unsuspecting Pythagoras had just climbed through the cat flap in the backdoor and was padding down the hallway towards his favourite armchair where he liked to nap. The house had a horrible smell, and the corridor was misty and dark. The cat didn't like it; he sneezed loudly.

On reaching the bottom of the stairs, his large yellow eyes gazed upwards. To his surprise, he spotted Nep's aunt sitting bolt upright on the landing. She looked startled and strange. But then, with a loud sigh, she seemed to faint or collapse, falling backwards heavily onto the floorboards.

Before long, she was snoring again, each breath making his feline body shake.

Then Pythagoras noticed something else. The eerie outline of a person was hovering in the air above the large, sleeping woman. The blue-grey shape looked a bit like a rain cloud or a spiral of smoke. Pythagoras decided it was a threat and arched his back.

But the confused cat could only watch in disbelief as the shadowy figure stretched into the shape of a long viper that came slithering down the stairs towards him. It felt like an icy mist rolling in off the marshes. Pythagoras was about to turn tail and run for the backdoor when the cloud surrounded him completely. He hissed loudly, but the darkness smothered him.

Within seconds, Pythagoras felt cold and stiff. He wanted to escape, but he couldn't move. Then it became difficult to breathe, and to hear, as plumes of ominous cloud drifted into his nostrils, mouth and ears.

When the air in the hall finally cleared, Pythagoras's eyes contained a dark glint – some kind of evil spark had lit itself within him. His eyes narrowed, as if devising a terrible plan. Then he opened his mouth, put his head back and yowled. It was an unearthly sound. Momentarily, the noise stirred Aunt Morgana, whose skin had returned to its usual healthy colour and whose eyes no longer looked hollow.

Suddenly, a decision had been reached. Within a few bounds, Pythagoras had reached the cat flap and leapt outside.

CHAPTER 6: THE MIDNIGHT MEETING OF FUR AND FEATHER

Just before midnight, Nep awoke in the Fish House to the flicker of candlelight and the imposing voice of Merlin the Globbatrotter:

> "In the shadow of the night,
> when magick starts to spark,
> creatures of fur and feather
> shall gather in the dark."

Dramatically, he flung his arms wide, before continuing:

> "When the moonlight glints above,
> beasties band together
> and animal languages
> become clear forever."

As the echo of his voice subsided, Merlin sat down and waited... and waited... and waited some more.

"It's been a terrible long time," he complained, "but I be's sure I got it right. I's been practising over and over." He twiddled his meaty thumbs nervously. "I wonder where they be? I be's sure I got it right and proper."

Still, Merlin and Nep waited.

"I reckon I'd better be trying again," said the globbatrotter eventually, and he clambered to his feet. Clearing his throat, he proclaimed, this time even louder:

"In the shadow of the night,
when magick starts to spark,
creatures of fur and feather–"

"Alright, alright, no need to shout," came a gentle country voice.

Something silky and soft was sliding through the hole in the back wall. Nep could just make out its fur. It looked like an otter, and he was surprised he could understand what it was saying.

"Oh, hello, Mistress Otter," said Merlin, hurrying to put his waistcoat back on. "Thank you mostings kindly for coming." He bowed politely.

"Is this the boy? Arthur Pendragon's child?" asked the otter.

"It is indeedy."

"Why so small?"

"Well, that be a long story," sighed the globbatrotter.

Nep wanted to say he was Bob's child, not Arthur Pendragon's (whoever that was), but he was too scared to open his mouth; the otter, with her dark, twinkling eyes, stood higher than his head.

"Heron is waiting outside," said the otter. "He can't fit through the hole."

"Well, I had better be opening the door, then," said Merlin, circling his shoulders and flexing his muscles.

His bulky frame hobbled over to the wooden door and he grasped it with both hands. Then, heaving with all his might, the door creaked and strained until it was open.

"Do come in, Sir Heron," said Merlin, bowing again.

An enormous grey heron stepped into the room on legs like stilts. It was ten times taller than

Merlin, and its huge beak looked like a deadly weapon, capable of slicing them in two in seconds.

"Greetings, Merlin the Globbatrotter," the bird said in an elderly, ponderous voice.

By this time, Nep was sitting bolt upright beside the wall, keeping very quiet and still. To his amazement, a beautiful white swan waddled into the room behind the heron. It was the size of a brachiosaurus, its long neck curling above the heads of everyone.

"A pleasure to be seeing you, Lord Swan," said Merlin, bowing once more.

"The pleasure is mine, I can assure you," said the majestic swan, nodding in reply.

"And where is the last of us?" enquired the heron.

"Well, young Neptune Trout, son of Arthur, be over there," replied Merlin, pointing in Nep's direction.

Again, Nep didn't dare to correct him.

"No, no, I'm referring to another creature of these marshes," said the heron.

"Oh, there be no frogs a-coming because this be a Meeting of Fur and Feather only," explained Merlin. "I believe that be stated in the regu... regu... regularations. Though I be sure the good frogs will be on our side, should the time come. What they lack in intellect, they do make up for in keenness."

"Yes, nothing wanting but the mind," smiled the swan.

"I don't think he means frogs," said the otter. "I think he means Margot."

"Margot?" said the bemused globbatrotter.

"The new collie," said Mistress Otter, "from the farm at the edge of the village."

"She's a young sheepdog in training," added the swan. "I believe she lives in the barn."

"Yes, she's one of us now," nodded the heron. "We must move with the times, you know."

"Oh... will Margot be a-coming here?" asked Merlin anxiously. "I have to admit, I be ever so slightly afeared of dogs."

Sir Heron chuckled deeply. "You don't need to fear Margot. Yes, she's a little enthusiastic–"

"One might even say boisterous," said Lord Swan.

"Chaotic is what I'd call her," added Mistress Otter.

"Ah, I do believe she's here," said Heron, peering towards the hole in the back wall, where loud panting could be heard.

Frantic wriggling and squirming ensued.

"Do excuse me," said Margot, scratching at the ground and breathing hard. "Running late. So many interesting smells at this time of night. Got distracted. Do excuse me. Be with you in just a...." More wriggling. "Just a...." More squirming. "Moment!"

"The door is open, you know," muttered the otter.

Margot shot into the room like a cork out of a bottle. In fact, she arrived with such force that she knocked the globbatrotter clean off his feet.

"Do excuse me," said Margot again, bowing before the strange, pig-like creature.

"No problem," said Merlin, dusting himself down. "I supposes."

"Mmm, cheese!" grinned the black dog, sniffing the globbatrotter's bag. She wagged her tail enthusiastically, causing a strong breeze to blow around the Fish House.

Merlin wrapped a protective arm around his bag and pulled it closer to his chest.

"Do forgive me," said Margot, remembering her place.

"It is so nice to welcome you, Margot, to this historic meeting," said Lord Swan, bowing again.

Bowing seems to be very popular, thought Nep.

But Margot was trotting round the room distractedly, sniffing each crevice and corner.

"Oh, yuck! Deadly nightshade!" she snorted, adding shortly afterwards, "Ah, there you are!" with a broad smile.

At least Nep hoped the dog was smiling at him; her sharp teeth were glinting in the candlelight.

"A bit smaller than I'd imagined," said Margot, her black nose almost touching his head.

Nep gulped audibly.

"I think that be quite close enough, Missy Margot," said the globbatrotter.

"Oh, do excuse me," said Margot, arriving back in the centre of the room in a single bound.

"Now, let the meeting begin," announced the heron. "After all, the mid of the night is already upon us."

★

For a long time, the animals discussed the return of Morgan le Fay in hushed voices. They stood away from Nep, their backs turned towards him. Nep, still feeling anxious, remained close to the cold wall of the Fish House and didn't move.

"It be multitudinous years since she did last be causing mayhem in these 'ere parts," said Merlin.

"Many a year indeed," nodded the sagely heron.

"One finds it most disturbing," whispered Lord Swan.

"But could you be sure, Merlin?" asked the otter. "How do you know the boy wasn't dreaming the whole episode? Perhaps it was nothing more than a nightmare?"

"No, no, no," said Merlin, shaking his head. "Mistress Otter, I were there, you sees. I did be peeping through the swinging door while this very happenstance did be occurring. Ghastly mist, it did come a-creeping from Neptune's aunt as she were lying at the top of the stairs. It be almost like she were possessed by something mostings frightful. Mostings evil. It be taking her over and filling the house with thick, choking smog."

"Oh dear, oh dear, how awful," said Margot, her tail between her legs.

"And I did be hearing those terrible words," said Merlin gravely. "Those words of yore, what my ancestor Merlin the First did hear all those ages ago when King Arthur and Queen Guinevere did do battle most fierce with Morgan le Fay. The last words the sorceress did utter before everyone presumed her to be dead and gone."

"What words? What words?" asked Margot, her eyes as wide as saucers.

"You knows the ones, gentlemen," said Merlin, nodding at Heron and Swan.

"I believe we do," said the heron, clearly shaken.

"Somethings about 'when the names are in place', and somethings else about 'story retold' and 'dark sorcery'. You knows the threat she spoke."

"I think you've said enough," warned Otter. "Those words must never be repeated by anyone kind or good or natural. They're words of pure evil."

"Indeed," said the swan pensively.

"Well, I be saying no more…" said Merlin. "But all I be's saying is that those be the words what be spoken by the dark mist what did creep from that poor woman's body."

"And there was laughter," said Nep quietly. The words had popped out of his mouth before he could stop them.

The creatures of fur and feather turned to look at him.

"Indeed?" enquired the heron.

"But it didn't sound like my aunt's laughter," said Nep. "I think Merlin the Globbatrotter's right; I think Aunt Morgana may have been possessed by an evil spirit. I only hope she's still alive. She looked… she looked…"

"Poor love," said the otter, staring at the boy's pale, troubled face.

"It is said the evil sorceress can control whichever living being she chooses," said the heron, lowering his voice and speaking to the group gathered around the candle. "She can inhabit one form and then cast it off and choose another."

The animals tutted and shook their heads, while Margot remained uncharacteristically quiet and still.

"Poor love," said Otter again. "Look how shaken he is."

She skittered over to where Nep was sitting and lay down beside him, wrapping her strong tail around his tiny body for comfort. And, for the first time in his life, Nep was enveloped in otter warmth and love.

"So, the plan is agreed then," said Lord Swan decisively. "To the waterways it is."

"Yeah, the multitudinous rhynes of the marshes," said Merlin, trying not to sound daunted or scared. "It is what Bob hisself did be requesting, if ever the vile sorceress did return – that I be hiding his beloved son in the complexicated waters of Avalon."

"We'll give you whatever protection we can," said the heron. "I can fly overhead, to watch out for the enemy, while Lord Swan can swim ahead of you to ensure the way is clear."

"I'll be nearby too, whenever possible," said Otter, curling her tail more tightly around Nep. "I have babes of my own to care for; I must feed them often so they'll grow healthy and strong. But I'll help you when I can."

"Thank you, Mistress Otter," said Heron.

"What about me?" said Margot, obviously unsettled. "I think the farmer will notice if I'm gone, you know. If I'm not there to round up the sheep, and nip the cows, and lick the children, and chase the chickens – oh, I shouldn't have mentioned that one – the farm will descend into disorder, then chaos, and ultimately despair, and *no one* can predict what will happen after that. It could be the end of farming as we know it."

Heron laughed to himself.

"There, there, Margot. No need to worry. We'll come and get you, if you're needed."

"Very good, very good," said Margot, her tail flicking with relief.

"But must we travel all the way to the Tor?" asked Lord Swan.

"That be where the antidote is, you sees," said the globbatrotter. "In the old dwelling place of King Arthur. It be the only land where it do grow."

"Such a dangerous journey for two small souls," said Mistress Otter, her worried gaze flitting between Merlin and Nep. "There are eels and grass snakes in those marshes, you know. Under no circumstances must you fall in the water."

"Yeah, I be mostings aware of the dangers," said Merlin. "My kind be not having the ability to swim – or float even. But the Quacking Nancy be a reliable craft and I be a master of navigation." He puffed out his chest proudly.

The animals glanced at each other and smiled.

"Brave soul," murmured the swan.

"But what of the message?" asked Otter, who never missed a detail.

"Ah, yes, the written message," said Heron. "I'd forgotten that momentarily. Merlin, if I'm to take your note to Arthur Pendragon, then I fear I'll be unable to accompany you on your voyage to Glastonbury."

"I be thinking it mostings urgent to be delivering that letter to the boy's father," said Merlin, shuffling anxiously from foot to foot. "Arthur must be informed of this terrible happenstance. I did explain to him that when his own father did choose those names of old, it were dreadful unwise. But he did laugh and think it some kind of jest – a pretty assemblage of names historical – but I knew, I knew. I did feel dread creeping through my globbatrotter bones. Such a dark history of sorcery is not one to be a-playing with. I did tell him. I did try. That is when Arthur did ask me to hide his boy, if danger ever came."

"Such a lack of foresight," said the swan, shaking his regal head from side to side.

"It seems I won't be joining you for a little while, then," said Heron, bowing once more to the company of creatures. "Do take care of your dear selves. Meanwhile, I'll begin the Ancient Sky Journey to Ring the Globe. It hasn't been attempted for many a century, but I'll carry the letter as far as I'm able. Then, one brave soul by one brave soul, my avian brothers and sisters will continue the journey I have begun, until the letter reaches the boy's father at Sagarmārthā in the highest reaches of the world."

Margot's ears pricked up.

"Where's that?" she asked eagerly.

"I believe it is the Nepalese name for Mount Everest," replied Lord Swan. "It means 'Peak of Heaven'. It is the highest mountain of all."

Margot's eyes grew round with wonder.

"No bird can fly that high!" snorted the otter. "How can a bird fly as high as heaven? It's impossible."

"I believe one bird can – well, according to legend," said Sir Heron.

"Which bird? Which bird?" asked Margot, almost bursting with excitement.

"The bar-headed goose," said the heron. "Or so I'm told."

"The what?" scoffed Otter. "Never heard of it!"

"Of course, it may only be a myth," said the old heron, "but we must try to reach Arthur, if we can."

"Look," said Nep, finally plucking up courage to speak his mind, "my dad's called Bob. Bob Trout.

Not Arthur. Not Pendragon. Just Bob. There must be some kind of mistake."

"Your father's full name be Robert Arthur Pendragon Trout," said Merlin. "He be not liking the formal tone of it, so he be telling everyone to call him Bob. Just like you be preferring Ned to Neptune when you be with your pals. Don't be thinking I haven't heard you playing in the garden," he chortled. "It be somewhats deafening at times."

"Robert Arthur Pendragon Trout?" said Nep, bewildered. "And what's Pendragon supposed to mean?"

"Head or chief dragon," replied the heron. "Though it really means 'chief warrior or leader'. It was the title of the first Arthur, the king after whom your father is named."

Nep looked completely puzzled.

"Don't worry," said Mistress Otter. "He's still Bob to you, my love, and that's fine."

"And to most people," said the heron.

"Now, returning to the Ancient Sky Journey to Ring the Globe – is it even possible, old friend?" asked the swan, turning to Sir Heron.

"It simply can't be," said Otter, shaking her silky head. "Flying around the whole world would be far too taxing and dangerous for any bird – even for a whole flock of birds. Never mind flying up to heaven!"

"Apparently, it was accomplished long ago, or so I'm told. And it's at times of great danger that we birds pull together. I won't fail you, Merlin the Globbatrotter," said Sir Heron with grim determination.

"Thank you mostings sincerely," said Merlin, his growly voice breaking with emotion. He took the folded piece of parchment from his bag and handed it to the wise old bird. "Good luck," he said, placing it carefully in the heron's long beak. "I be mostings obliged." Then Merlin the Globbatrotter bowed so low, his snout almost touched the earthen floor.

CHAPTER 7: THE QUEST BEGINS

Robert Arthur Pendragon Trout, commonly known as Bob, was feeling on top of the world – almost literally! He loved Nepal – the smell of woodsmoke in the air, the bustling, vibrant streets, and the gracious people who were always friendly. How he'd missed the place!

The last time he'd visited Nepal was when Neptune was only an infant; dear Gwen had agreed to stay behind in Somerset to look after their son while Bob searched for rare plants in this rugged, mountainous land. Bob's sister, Morgana, had kindly offered to help her. Tragically, Gwen had died while he'd been abroad. He would never have left her if he'd known how frail she must have been.

The flight had taken almost eighteen hours to reach Kathmandu, the capital city of Nepal. Luckily, though, Bob had perfected the art of 'switching off'; he could easily forget that anyone and everyone existed, if he put his mind to it. So, with the bands *Procol Harum* and *Jefferson Airplane* playing in the earphones of his old Walkman, he'd slept comfortably on the plane for many, many hours.

On arriving in the sprawling city of Kathmandu with its ancient, dusty streets, Bob had felt instantly at home. Grinning from ear to ear, he'd sauntered past the colourful markets and headed towards Durbar Square. He could never resist a visit to this beautiful place with its plazas and water fountains, and its red-tiled, towering pagodas.

"Peace, man!" said Bob, with a smile and a wave, to anyone who passed by.

But Bob still had a bus journey of 188 kilometres ahead of him, to the pretty town of Jiri, located among green hills and woodland – the gateway to Sagarmārthā or Mount Everest. As it was a pleasant and unusually dry day in early August, he opted to sit on the roof rack of the bus, to breathe in the fresh air of the high plateaus and to marvel at the majestic scenery.

Before long, he'd be enjoying the Himalayan foothills – crossing suspended bridges over raging rivers, creeping past yak trains, admiring tiny villages shrouded in the scent of peat smoke, and pausing at Buddhist shrines called chortens.

He inhaled deeply, feeling completely at peace. All was well with the world.

★

Before beginning their own quest, Merlin the Globbatrotter asked for the Quacking Nancy and his trusty knitting needle to be brought to him beside Meare's closest waterway. He and Nep simply didn't have the strength to trudge back to Ghost House to retrieve the large rubber duck and drag it all the way to the riverbank. They also didn't want to encounter Morgan le Fay or her army of toads.

Eager to help, Margot and Mistress Otter raced through the inky night to Ghost House's overgrown garden. All was quiet; nobody was there. So, making barely a splash, Otter slipped into the pond under the willow tree and re-emerged beside the Quacking Nancy. Carefully, she bit through the string that held it in place, then pushed the duck towards the edge of the pond with her dainty nose.

Meanwhile, Margot was becoming acquainted with Norman the garden gnome. At first the small figure with the fixed smile had made her jump, but now she was sniffing around his alabaster feet and face, wagging her tail with excitement.

"How do you do? How do you do?" she said.

"Here, take this," said Otter, "and I'll grab the needle."

"Do excuse me," said Margot to Norman.

The collie gently picked up the rubber duck by its head and carried it in her large mouth. Meanwhile, Otter climbed onto the tea tray, making it wobble madly, and grasped the knitting needle in her small, sharp teeth.

Then, as silent as the night that shrouded them, they bounded back to the Abbot's Fish House and the river beyond, where Merlin, Nep and the two large birds were waiting patiently.

"I had no idea it were to be a river and not a rhyne," said Merlin, his legs visibly shaking. "Though it be straight and somewhats calm, this be much bigger than what I be's expecting. There be some eddies... nay, swirling... and great murkiness to its depth," he said, staring into the deep, dark water. "I have nearly drownded once in my life, and I be not wanting to do it again."

"But, my dear friend, the River Brue is the most direct route to Glastonbury," said Lord Swan.

He explained to Merlin and Nep that the River Brue ran south-east for approximately four miles, eventually reaching the southern fringes of the town. From there, it would be almost a mile's walk north to St Michael's Tower on its famous hill, known as Glastonbury Tor.

Sir Heron put down the piece of parchment and gazed up into the brightening sky.

"At dawn, I'll fly east," he said. "Not far from the great city of London, with all its noise and bustle, I'm told there's a friendly flock of pigeons. I'm sure one of those knowledgeable birds will help me. All creatures of feather know the legend of the Ancient Sky Journey, and they're duty-bound to assist."

"You'll never reach London, Sir Heron," said Otter, looking worried. "You're not as young as you used to be, you know. And you're a country bird."

"I'll journey as far as I can," said the heron, "and when I can fly no further, I'll seek help."

"Do take care," said Lord Swan apprehensively. "One has heard tales of massive metal birds, a thousand times greater than any swan, that sweep through the air and devour all in their path."

"Yes, I've heard of those too," said the heron. "I'll be wary. I'll fly low for as long as I'm able."

"But I've heard of men who carry a machine in their hands – a metal snake with a bite more vicious than any adder. One strike and you'll be no more, Sir Heron," said Otter.

Nep was beginning to feel uncomfortable; sometimes humankind made him despair.

"I've heard of those also," said the heron. "Trust me, I'll travel with caution. And you, my dear friends, will be with me as I fly – in spirit at least."

"Good journeying to you, Sir Heron," said Merlin. "'Parting be such sweet sorrow'[6], as the Bard hisself did say. Thank you mostings kindly for helping us."

"Thank you, Sir Heron," said Nep, and he bowed his head respectfully to the massive bird.

"Dear boy," said the heron.

"Right then," said Merlin, mustering all his courage, "we bests be off."

"It is a most courageous thing that you're doing for the child," whispered the swan into Merlin's ear. "Especially after what happened to your own dear family. Arthur Pendragon would be so grateful if he knew. And so proud."

"'Thank me no thankings, nor proud me no prouds',"[7] replied Merlin modestly.

The otter picked up the knitting needle and passed it to the globbatrotter, who strapped a broad leaf to its end with a piece of grass to create a paddle. Then, when he was ready, Margot dropped the Quacking Nancy into the water with a splash. Mistress Otter dived into the river and held the boat in place beside the bank while Merlin and Nep carefully boarded the bobbing yellow duck.

"Hold fast now," said the otter, as she gently but firmly pushed the little vessel into the centre of the river.

"I'm afraid the current flows in the opposite direction to Glastonbury," said the swan, "so you'll need to paddle hard, my friend."

"Oh wonderful," sighed the globbatrotter, rolling his piggy eyes.

"If it's too much for you, you can always ride on my back," offered the swan. "There will be no shame in that."

"Excuses I," said Merlin with indignation, "the Quacking Nancy and I have been through many scrapes together, and globbatrotters be known for their impressive strength."

"Of course," said the swan. "Of course."

As the first light of dawn painted the sky and river the palest pink, the Quacking Nancy jolted into motion, and the two intrepid sailors held on tight as Mistress Otter nudged them through the water, creating a V-shaped wake as she swam.

"Good luck," panted Margot, wagging her tail. "Good luck, good luck!"

With that, she turned and charged back towards the farm before daylight woke the farmer and betrayed her absence.

Lord Swan ruffled his tail feathers and launched himself into the water with a dramatic swoosh. Then, silently and gracefully, he glided along beside Mistress Otter and the Quacking Nancy, turning his periscope head from side to side to peer into the long grass on either bank.

"Farewell," he whispered to Heron as they drifted down the river.

The stooped, grey figure of the heron watched the small party sail away.

"Farewell, my friends," he breathed. "Farewell."

CHAPTER 8: THE RIVER BRUE

The day was turning into a beautiful one, and the bright sun shimmered on the water like a million stars. A passing dragonfly frightened Nep, making him duck sharply. He hadn't realised how ferocious their faces were, or how large their eyes were, or how powerful their jaws were. Even its lacy wings made an ominous humming sound. But luckily the dragonfly wasn't interested in a bright yellow duck with reins tied around its bill, or the duck's passengers; it had small insects to chase and devour.

By mid-morning, and a mile along the River Brue, Mistress Otter apologised and explained she'd have to leave them for a while. She needed to swim back to her cubs to feed them; they'd be hungry and wondering where she was.

"Will you be okay without me?" she asked, worried.

"Please do not concern yourself, Mistress Otter," said the swan. "I will remain with Merlin and Neptune, come what may. You are a parent and must attend to your young."

"I'll be back as soon as I can, I promise," said the otter, whirling around in the bright water and vanishing beneath the surface.

But as soon as she'd gone, Merlin felt the strain of paddling. Though the surface of the river looked smooth and glassy, its current was deceptively strong. He put his back into it, working hard with his makeshift paddle, but his muscles ached and sweat trickled down his ginger face.

"Oh dear, oh dear," he muttered, glancing down into the water from time to time.

"Excuse me," said Nep as politely as he could, "I think we're going backwards."

"No, I still be's paddling forwards," panted the determined globbatrotter.

"Yes, you're paddling forwards, but we're not actually getting anywhere," said Nep.

"No, no, we be making fair progress," said Merlin, flushed and breathless.

"But we were opposite that fence post a moment ago," said Nep, pointing ahead of them, "and now it's a long way off."

Suddenly, the Quacking Nancy spun around in the water and starting bobbing back the way they'd come.

"Oh dear, oh dear," cried the globbatrotter. "This be somewhats upsettifying."

The rubber duck was swaying violently as it hurried back down the river, and Nep and Merlin had to cling on to the reins.

"Perhaps you should accept my offer of assistance now?" suggested the calm swan as he glided back to join them. "You're both welcome to travel on my back. I can assure you, it's soft and comfortable. You may even be able to rest for a while."

"That does sound like a good idea," said Nep. They hadn't slept in a very long time.

"But what about the Quacking Nancy?" cried Merlin. "I be's not abandoning her in these perilous waters. That would be mostings ungrateful, and foolhardy too."

"Let me look for a safe spot to moor her," said the patient swan. "I'm sure we could conceal her until we travel this way again. How about over there?" He pointed with his beak towards some tall reeds at the water's edge.

"Oh, I don't know, I don't know..." said the globbatrotter.

"I think it might be a good idea, Merlin," said Nep gently. "You've done well to come this far, but it'll take us ages to reach Glastonbury if we don't accept a ride from the swan."

"Oh, very well," sighed Merlin. "I supposes we must."

Lord Swan pushed the little craft into the thick of the reeds and hid the knitting needlle.

"I do's be hoping we can be finding her again," said Merlin, close to tears.

"I'm sure she'll be okay," whispered Nep, patting the globbatrotter kindly on the shoulder.

Clutching onto their supplies, they clambered off the rubber duck and onto Lord Swan's back, instantly feeling the latent power of the great bird's body.

"Do settle down and enjoy the voyage," said the swan.

So, the two friends lay down among the silky feathers, grateful that they could finally rest.

As they sailed out of the reeds and into the river, Merlin glanced back at the rubber duck and whispered, "Oh, my dearest Quacking Nancy. I be's so sorry." He sniffed loudly and then shut his eyes. Sleep was finally a possibility.

★

"Merlin, I'm so confused," said Nep.

It was early afternoon, and Nep and the globbatrotter were sharing a piece of cheese and a few bits of cracker as they made their way upriver on Lord Swan's back.

"I think that be the natural state of most human beans," mused Merlin. "Except for the likes of Norman, of course. But he be's a deep and impressive thinker. The restings of 'em do likes to be speaking and not to be thinking mostings of the time."

"Quite so," said the wise swan as he paddled gracefully on. "By the way, please be careful not to drop any crumbs on my feathers. I do like to look my best, you know."

"Oh, of coursings," said the globbatrotter, frantically swishing crumbs into the river.

"But I'm confused about everything," continued Nep. "My aunt, for example. What happened to her? Is she alive? And my family's names. I mean, why should Dad be named after King Arthur or Pendragon or whoever he is? And why have I never heard of a globbatrotter before? Are there any other globbatrotters? I really don't know what's going on."

There was a long pause.

"That certainly be's a lot of confusion. Let us be starting with globbatrotters," said Merlin, "because that be the mostings important and interesting part. Though, I must be confessing, it be a long story. I be's not knowing where to start."

"Start at the beginning, dear Merlin," advised the swan.

And so Merlin did.

"Well... firstings, I should be explaining that we globbatrotters be ancient creatures of history and legend, originating from these marshes what you do be calling the Somerset Levels. We be creatures of the wetlands, you sees, who be using the ancient Sweet Track, long-forgotten villages and rhynes to be getting about. We be stealthy – nay, almostings invisible – among the reeds and watery ways."

"Oh, I think Dad's told me about the Sweet Track," said Nep. "Isn't it an old wooden path through the marshes, built in the Stone Age?"

"That be right, young Neptune. There be multitudinous wooden trackways criss-crossing everywheres, and there be lake villages from the Iron Age too. These be our mostings secret and special places. In fact, for many generations, my family did be living at an ancient lake village near Westhay. It were mostings pleasant indeed." The globbatrotter's eyes sparkled with enthusiasm as he talked about his old life.

"So, how did you end up on your own, Merlin?"

"That be a sad and fearsome tale what did be happening about a decade ago. Your father did be finding me, nearly drownded in the rhynes, and he be taking me home to Meare and hiding me in the abandoned house. Then he be giving me the Tea & Biscuit to live in. Sometimes he be feeding me on icing buns," he said, licking his lips. "I be rather partial to icing buns, and I do loves and respects your father mostings highly."

"But what happened? How did you nearly drown?"

"Well, it were a terrible day of rain, and more rain, and yet more rain. It be like a torrent gushing down. All the marshes did be getting flooded. Everywheres be underwater; there be no dry land at all. Even the huge houses of the human personages did be getting waterlogged. And, as you knows, globbatrotters be not known for their great height or their swimming skills. It were mighty dangerous – nay, it were deadly."

"I'm sorry, Merlin. Did you get separated from your family?" asked Nep.

Merlin sighed deeply. "Indeedy I did. There be Aeriene, my beautiful wife with rosy cheeks and curly hair, and my little nippers Edla and Merlin Lefwinus. I do miss 'em so awful badly. Not to mention my brothers and sisters and nieces and nephews. And other globbatrotter families too. They all be gone." His eyes filled with sudden tears that glinted behind his thick glasses, and his shoulders shook as he sobbed.

"Oh, Merlin, that's awful." Nep shuffled closer and tried to put his arm around his friend – though the globbatrotter's back was very broad.

"I'm so sorry, my dear friend," whispered the swan tenderly.

Through sniffs and snuffles, Merlin said, "At the time, some globbatrotters did be saying they would try to reach high ground. Tor Hill be the only place visible, but it be so many miles off and everywhere be flooded. Our little rafts would never be reaching such a far-off spot. Then we all got separated and I never be seeing them again. They all be drownded in the flood."

"Didn't Dad ever take you there?" asked Nep. "To Glastonbury? To see if anyone had survived?"

Merlin's lips were trembling and his voice was shaking.

"Well, I believe he did be finding a few globbatrotter bodies sometime laterwhiles, you sees, floating in the rhynes, all drownded and deadified. But he be not showing me; it be too upsettifying. Of course, he be giving them a proper burial an' all."

Nep shook his head sadly.

"Bob also be saying that Glastonbury be so busy now-days, with motorcars and omnibuses and multitudinous personages, that no globbatrotter could ever have been making it to the Tor alive."

Nep gulped loudly.

"Do you think we'll make it, Merlin?" he asked, realising the magnitude of the task that lay ahead of them.

"Well, we can but try, young'un," said Merlin. "In fact, I owe it to Bob to makes sure we does. He saved I; now I must be saving you."

A shadow danced across their faces then, out of nowhere, a huge marsh harrier appeared in the sky. It dived down at them, its dagger-like talons outstretched and ready.

"Duck!" shouted Lord Swan.

"No, I think that be a bird of prey," said the globbatrotter, standing up and peering into the sun.

"Get down!" yelled Nep, grabbing the globbatrotter around the legs and tackling him.

The harrier streaked overhead, the sound of its feathers whistling in their ears, and its claws just missed them. But now Merlin was dangling over the side of the swan's back. Flailing wildly, he tried to clutch onto something to stop himself sliding off altogether. But, before Nep could grab him, the globbatrotter, squealing loudly, splashed into the river.

"Helps I!" he shrieked as he thrashed about, trying to keep his head above water.

"Oh no! Globbatrotters can't swim," said Nep, frantically trying to reach Merlin's hand.

"I'll get him," said Lord Swan, paddling round in the water.

But the current had already carried Merlin away from them, and now his bristly head was disappearing underwater. Worse still, Nep could see a large eel, a glint of silver, wriggling through the water, heading straight for Merlin. Its cold, black eyes were fixed on him and its mouth was opening.

"Do something!" screamed Nep.

The swan stretched down into the river with his long neck, while Nep tried to peer into the watery depths.

"It's no good," gasped the swan, coming up for air. "He sank too quickly. I can't reach him – not with you on my back."

Nep was just about to dive off the swan's back when he spotted something else in the water – something sleek and brown and swift.

"It's the otter!" he cried.

Like a torpedo, Mistress Otter shot towards the eel and bit into its long, smooth body, killing it instantly. Then she circled round and dived deeper, positioning herself between the globbatrotter and the bottom of the river. Just as Merlin was about to land on the muddy riverbed, he found himself on the otter's back instead and, in an instant, they were swimming up towards daylight.

Using his strong beak, Lord Swan took hold of the globbatrotter by his waistcoat, then reached round and placed the drenched creature on his downy back.

"Merlin! Speak to me!" cried Nep tearfully. "Merlin, are you okay? Merlin!"

The globbatrotter was pale and motionless.

"Roll him over," spluttered the otter, still holding the eel in her mouth, "so the water can flow out of him."

With a huge effort, Nep pushed against the globbatrotter's side until eventually he rolled over onto his front. Immediately, Merlin started coughing.

"Thank goodness," sighed the swan. "And thank goodness you arrived when you did, Mistress Otter."

The otter was lying on her back in the water, munching on the eel.

"And I got a meal out of it too," she grinned between mouthfuls.

"Oh dear, oh dear," said a dripping Merlin as he hauled himself up to a sitting position and looked around, dazed. "We globbatrotters not be known for our swimming skills."

"You gave us quite a fright, old friend," said the swan.

"I'm so sorry, Merlin. It was all my fault," said Nep, still crying. "I tackled you and you fell into the water."

"Don't be so ridiculous, young sir," said the globbatrotter. "You did be saving I from that scary duck."

CHAPTER 9: THE AMBUSH

The long, straight river looked like a slice of heaven. Merlin, Nep and Lord Swan were mesmerised by the blue sky and white puffy clouds that were reflected in its waters; it was like drifting through a summer sky. Midges and other insects thronged above them, while a few fish rose to the surface of the water, causing rings to spiral outwards hypnotically. The River Brue was well known for its fishing; anglers could catch perch, bream, roach, rudd, chub, eel, pike and sometimes even carp here. Nep tried not to look too closely, though, because compared to his size, some of the fish looked as big as sharks. And, if truth be told, he was still shaken after Merlin's accident.

Across the hazy, flat countryside, the three friends could make out the steep hill and tower of Glastonbury Tor. It was a landmark that could be seen for miles around Somerset's heartlands. But it still looked worryingly distant, and the chances of reaching it and finding the antidote seemed minuscule.

All the while, Mistress Otter ran happily along the river's edge, crashing through tall grasses and occasionally disappearing from sight to stop and chew a crunchy beetle or juicy slug.

It was a warm, sleepy afternoon and Lord Swan was feeling weary.

"Would you mind if we were to pause and rest for a while?" he asked. "I must have swum at least two miles and, I have to admit, my legs are rather tired."

"Why, of coursings not," said Merlin, whose clothes were still soggy. "Please stop, my friend, and be resting yourself. Nep and I will be keeping a lookout."

"Perhaps we should stop over there?" suggested Nep, pointing towards the riverbank. "It might be safer than drifting in the river."

"Quite so," nodded the swan. "We don't want either of you falling in the water again, do we?"

The swan paddled to the water's edge and wedged himself among a patch of marsh marigolds, his tail feathers towards the bank. As he lay his large head across his back and closed his eyes, Merlin and Nep shuffled backwards towards his tail. Soon the swan was sleeping comfortably.

"Merlin?" whispered Nep. "Why do globbatrotters live near water if they can't swim? It seems so dangerous."

"Well, in the days of yore, we did be using the many tracks and pathways of the marshes to be getting about. It were only laterwhiles, as the water levels did be rising, that we had to learn to fashion rafts and boats."

"I see," said Nep.

"But we did become great boatmen and navigators, to be sure. We be sailing for many generations now."

Nep smiled, then he and the globbatrotter settled down quietly to allow Lord Swan to sleep. However, it seemed Merlin got bored very quickly.

"Did I be telling you that globbatrotters be living for a long time?" he said. "Guess how old I be, Neptune. Go on, guess."

"I have no idea," whispered Nep. "Maybe... I don't know, forty?"

Merlin laughed heartily. "We globbatrotters be living for two hundred years or more, and I be almost exactly one hundred and fifty-two."

"No!"

"Oh yes," chuckled Merlin, his hooter crinkling endearingly. "And, of course, I be Merlin the Eighth. Afore me there were Merlin the Seventh. And afore he, there were... let me see, um... Merlin the Sixth. And afore he, there were... um, now that would be... Merlin the Fifth."

Nep drifted off for a few moments.

"Taking us right back to Merlin the First, you sees – my very first ancestor, who be that mostings famous assistant to Arthur Pendragon hisself."

Forgetting that Lord Swan was dozing, Nep laughed out loud.

"You mean, Merlin the wizard, King Arthur's magician, was a globbatrotter?"

"Well, you don't be thinking that Merlin be a human bean, does you? That would be mostings ridiculous!"

"Of course he was a human bean... I mean, a human being," said Nep.

"Well, how do you think the first Merlin did be performing spells and magick, and be knowing about worts and potions? Those be not human skills. Those be the skills of globbatrotters."

"But that's crazy! My dad knows everything there is to know about herbs and potions."

"Yeah, and that be because I did be teaching he," replied Merlin.

"Merlin the magician was a man!" said Nep, getting cross.

Merlin the Eighth looked offended.

"I never be hearing anything so witless in all my days outs and ins. I mean, were you there in those days of old? Did you be a-witnessing Merlin the First with your very own twinkle-eyes?"

"Of course not," said Nep.

"Well then," said the globbatrotter, as if that settled matters. "You human beans be liking to take the credit for everything in the whole widing world, but we globbatrotters be the noble wizards of legend. It be in our blood."

Without opening his eyes, Lord Swan sighed wearily.

"So, can you do spells then?" asked Nep.

"I did be doing spells in the Fish House," said Merlin. "You were there, and you can now understand creature speak."

"But how do I know that was you? Maybe I just learned how to understand animals on my own. Maybe it's a gift."

"You be talking rot," huffed the globbatrotter.

"Well, do some magic tricks, then. Go on, show me what you can do."

"Bob be saying that I must not be doing no magick or–"

"Well, that's convenient, isn't it?" said Nep, folding his arms.

The swan cleared his long throat.

"Excuses I," said Merlin, "but Bob be telling me not to be drawing attention to myself. He not be wanting anyone to find me. Magick be only for the mostings dire emergencies, he be saying."

"Yeah, yeah," said Nep.

"Perhaps a slightly more respectful tone?" suggested the tired swan. "Globbatrotters are well known for their wizardry, you know."

Nep decided to ignore them both and stare into the distance.

★

Sir Heron, exhausted and aching, had just arrived in Reading, a town situated forty miles to the west of London. He'd caused many onlookers to point and gasp as he'd landed, rather clumsily, on the tall spire of the old town hall.

Despite his best efforts, though, the pigeons on the roof seemed to be particularly dim.

"Sorry, guv," cooed a grey pigeon, "we ain't never 'eard of any Ancient Sky Journey to Ring the Globe. You makin' it up or somefink?"

"Wot is 'e, anyway?" asked a pale pigeon. "'E's the funniest-looking gull I've ever seen."

"I can assure you, it's a famous journey, designed to help humankind," explained the heron. "The story of it has been passed down from generation to generation. In fact, *all* birds know of it – or at least they should."

"Well, we've just come from Laaandan and we don't know nuffink abaat it, mate," said the cocky grey bird, "so you can shove off."

A small pigeon stepped forward and tried to be more helpful.

"Most of us ain't got no families, see, governor, so we ain't never 'ad the benefit of bedtime stories an' all that. Maybe we just ain't been told abaat it?"

"Sorry we can't help you, Mr Gull," said the pale pigeon.

Wearily, the heron took off once more and flew towards the River Thames and Tower Hamlets. Perhaps the old ravens of the Tower of London would be better educated.

★

Merlin and Nep hadn't meant to doze off in the late-afternoon sun – they were supposed to be keeping watch – but they were about to pay the price for their mistake.

All of a sudden, toads appeared from everywhere. Lumbering, ugly creatures stumbled through the grass, slunk out of the water, and crept over the marsh marigolds.

"Merlin! Toads!" cried Nep, waking up with a jolt.

"Oh no," breathed the startled globbatrotter, "Morgan le Fay must be here."

The bleary-eyed swan looked up as dozens of toads clambered onto his back. "Get off!" he snapped, picking up toads with his beak and hurling them into the water. "Get off, I say!"

"Quick, Neptune, run!" said Merlin.

But it was too late; they were surrounded by lumpy toads with leering eyes.

"Jump onto the bank and try to get away," urged the swan, pecking at the toads to clear an escape route for his friends.

By now, toads were climbing over the swan's back and up his neck.

"Clear off, gundiguts!" shouted the globbatrotter, elbowing the creatures aside.

Somehow, Merlin and Nep managed to dodge between the toads and leap for the grassy bank, but more were waiting there.

"Where be Mistress Otter?" said Merlin, trying not to panic.

"I don't know," said Nep, terrified.

"Mistress Otter!" yelled Merlin, but she was nowhere to be seen.

By now, the poor swan was smothered in writhing, grey-green bodies. They were crawling down his legs, trying to pull him under the water.

"I must flee!" he cried.

Desperately, Lord Swan stretched his neck upwards and raised his body out of the water, flapping his huge wings to shake off the toads. Then he paddled frantically towards the middle of the river, with his wings beating hard. Racing across the surface of the water, he eventually managed to take off, as toad after toad fell from his legs, neck and back and plopped into the river.

"I'm sorry, my friends!" he called, glancing back towards Nep and Merlin as he flew into the distance. "I'm sorry!"

The two helpless friends watched him go. Then, to Nep's great surprise and relief, out of nowhere, Pythagoras appeared on the riverbank beside them.

"Pythagoras! How did you get here?" said Nep.

"Be that your prickle-claw?" asked Merlin suspiciously. "From Meare?"

"Yes," smiled Nep. "He must have come to save us."

The cat sauntered over, seemingly untroubled by the ranks of toads.

"It's me, Neptune!" said Nep, waving his tiny arms. "Look, it's me!" But the smile was fading from the boy's lips. Would the cat recognise him, or would he attack? And what was the cat doing here, halfway to Glastonbury?

"You be absolutely sure that be he?" asked Merlin nervously.

Meanwhile, the toads were shuffling backwards to allow the powerful, green-eyed

Jealousy to step forward. Sneering at Merlin and Nep, he signalled to the rest of the toads to create a great circle around the prisoners.

"Pythagoras?" said Nep. The cat's eyes seemed unfamiliar, even haunting; they were glowing midnight blue. "Is that you?"

Then suddenly Mistress Otter was tearing along the riverside towards them. She put her head down and rammed the cat with all her strength, sending several toads and Pythagoras flying into the long grass.

"No!" shouted Nep. "That's my cat!"

"That's no cat," said the otter, catching her breath. "That's something evil and most unnatural."

The cat got to his feet and glared at the otter, emitting hate with his every breath. Then a dark mist started to drift upwards from his fur, twining and twisting into the blue sky, billowing upwards, becoming thicker and darker.

"Oh no," breathed Nep, "not again."

There was no escape; they were surrounded by a wall of angry toads.

"It be her, the sorceress," whispered Merlin.

The brave otter tried once more to defeat the enemy. She jumped over the toads, charged towards the brown cat and ploughed into him, knocking him off his feet again. But now, even though Pythagoras was lying motionless in the grass, the fog continued to surge from every pore of his body, quickly forming into the shape of an imposing woman in a trailing gown. Then evil laughter filled the air, sending icy chills down Nep's spine.

Gradually, the cloud changed its form. It swirled round and round, creating a dizzying whirlwind that tore across the ground towards Mistress Otter. Nep and Merlin braced themselves against the blast. The whirlwind enveloped the otter's body, whisked her high up into the sky and then hurled her far across the marsh.

"*Nooooo!*" screamed Nep, distraught.

The otter shot through the air, like a cannonball fired from a cannon, and landed somewhere out of sight with a bone-breaking thud. Then silence.

As the swirling darkness gradually stopped spinning and reformed into the hazy shape of a woman, Nep glared at it.

"*I hate you!*" he screamed, furious and despairing. "*That otter was my friend!*"

The spiteful cackling began again, but soon it was followed by that eerie and familiar curse. This time, though, Morgan le Fay's voice had a smug, self-satisfied tone:

"When Arthur Pendragon
and gentle Guinevere
raise a babe to a child,
then Morgan will appear.
When the names are in place
and the story retold,
my power will return –
dark sorcery of old."

On Jealousy's command, the army of toads marched forwards and grabbed Merlin and Nep. Struggling and kicking, the globbatrotter and the tiny boy were dragged away across the marsh beneath the shadow of a mysterious, swirling mist.

★

At the edge of the moor, not far from the Abbot's Fish House, Mary and Jesh were playing football.

"Look at the sky!" cried Mary suddenly.

The two children stared in astonishment at the dark, churning clouds that swept across the distant Levels.

"I've never seen a storm like that," said Jesh. "Maybe it's a cyclone."

"Maybe a hurricane's coming this way!" said Mary.

"I don't like the look of it," said Jesh nervously. "Let's go home."

Mary and Jesh picked up their football and raced back towards their houses without even glancing back.

And, all the while, the elusive shape of an injured otter was hauling herself slowly and painfully over the tumps of grass back towards the refuge of the river.

CHAPTER 10: PRISONERS

To the tourists' amazement and delight, on the neatly mown lawns beside the high castle walls, a heron and raven stood side by side for quite some time – a sight never before witnessed at the Tower of London. The grey heron placed a folded piece of paper at the raven's feet. Perhaps the tall bird had brought it some kind of gift? The tourists laughed and took many photographs, thinking the behaviour of the birds was heart-warming and sweet.

Luckily for Sir Heron, the wise raven knew all about the Ancient Sky Journey to Ring the Globe, and he passed on some useful and detailed information.

"One feels a certain obligation to assist, Sir Heron," croaked the raven, "but I simply cannot leave the Tower. It's my duty to stay here. If the ravens of the Tower of London ever leave, then the monarchy and this country will undoubtedly fall."

"I quite understand, Earl Raven," bowed the heron, acknowledging the raven's serious position. "But if you can't help me, do you know of anyone else who can? A young boy is in danger and we need to find his father who's climbing Mount Everest, the highest mountain in the world. He must return to Somerset immediately."

"I see," said the raven. "Well, I do know a gull who regularly fishes in the English Channel. Sometimes she even crosses the Channel to visit her relatives in France. I'm sure she would help us. I'll see what I can do in the morning."

"Thank you, Earl Raven."

"Of course, we'll have to involve the songbirds of Europe after that, for the next part of the journey."

"I only hope those little birds will be strong enough to carry the parchment," said Sir Heron. "Those tiny beaks and dainty wings – how ever will they manage?"

"It's not just the weight of the paper, or the distance of the journey," said the raven. "I hear that thousands and thousands of songbirds are trapped in nets in Europe every year. Humans can be so cruel to us."

The heron looked grief-stricken. "It's hard to comprehend suffering on such a scale."

"Perhaps a whole flock of birds could carry the parchment between them?" said the raven. "They could take it in turns to carry the message, to increase their chances of success."

"Yes, that might work."

"I'll ask the gull to suggest it to them. Then I believe the songbirds must try to locate the white stork of Ukraine. Such a beautiful bird – white and shining like a dove of peace, though even bigger than you, Sir Heron."

"What would be the best course of action after that, my wise friend?" asked the heron.

"From what I recall of the Ancient Sky Journey, the magnificent steppe eagle of Kazakhstan will take over from the stork and continue the quest. She will glide south towards Pakistan and the Himalayas. I'm sure the pretty chukar will help in Pakistan. But who will be strong enough and brave enough to fly to Mount Everest? Can any bird fly at such altitudes, Sir Heron? I certainly couldn't," said the shining black raven.

"Legend has it that the bar-headed goose is the one we need," said the heron. "I've heard that every spring, large flocks of these geese fly from India through the Himalayan Mountains, and over Mount Everest, on their way to their nesting grounds in Tibet, so it must be possible. It's the bar-headed goose that the chukar must find. I only hope the goose will make it."

"I hope they *all* will make it," said the raven solemnly. "For their sake, and for the sake of the boy."

★

When the whirling fog finally seemed to have gone, Lord Swan circled above the marshes for a long time, closely watching the direction of the toad army and trying to predict its destination. But toads travel slowly overland and the light was fading fast, so he flew back to Meare and landed near the farm. With brave Sir Heron flying to London and poor Mistress Otter probably dying or dead, there was no one else who could possibly help him.

The swan honked in the field next to the farmyard, and it wasn't long before an eager and speedy Margot arrived on the scene.

After the customary bowing, Lord Swan explained in detail what had happened.

"But wait for nightfall, Margot," he warned. "It's too dangerous to go in daylight. The sorceress will be waiting and watching, I'm sure, and she's too powerful for the likes of us. Being white, they'd spot me immediately, even in darkness; but you're almost completely black, so you may be able to sneak into their camp unseen."

"Yes, yes, I understand," said Margot, realising it would be down to her, and her alone, to save the boy and the globbatrotter. "I'll do my best. I'll try my very hardest. I certainly will."

"Thank you, Margot," said the swan, bowing his regal head again. "Your loyalty will not be forgotten."

"And if I hurry," panted the dog, "I'll be back before dawn. After all, if I'm not here to round up the sheep, and nip the cows, and lick the children, and chase the chickens... oh..."

"Yes, I seem to remember you mentioned that before. Something about disorder and chaos? But I'm sure all will be well."

"We can't be too careful, you know, Lord Swan," said Margot. "If I'm not home by morning–"

"I'm sure you'll be back in time to carry out your farmwork, Margot," said the swan. "Now, listen carefully while I give you directions."

"Yes, do tell me," said Margot. "I'm all ears. I'm ready and waiting. In fact, I'm paying attention with every fibre of my being. I won't miss a thing..."

The swan sighed.

★

It was the darkest hour of the night. Seated on the soggy ground, deep in the marshes of Avalon, Neptune and Merlin huddled together beneath a straggly willow tree. Their hands were tied tightly behind their backs with rope made of plaited grasses. Their legs were bound together too. They stood no chance of escape.

The toads had marched them to the man-made island or crannog between Glastonbury and the village of Godney – the site of another prehistoric settlement. This seemed to be the army's base, and Merlin and Nep had never seen so many toads in their lives. Warty bodies lay slumped everywhere, either grunting or snoring. Although toads are nocturnal animals, these were exhausted from the long trek to the lake village and they all seemed to be asleep.

"How come the toads don't speak?" whispered Nep. "I can understand the birds and the otter and the dog, but not the toads."

"Well, amphibians be not creatures of fur and feather, you sees," whispered Merlin. "So, when I did make my spell in the Fish House, toads were not included."

Nep still looked confused.

"Was that really you, then?"

"Of coursings it were."

"And will I always be able to understand animals? I mean, the ones with fur or feathers."

"Oh yeah," said Merlin casually. "It will take some practice, but as long as you concentrate mostings hard, their languages will become known to you – especially at night when it be quiet."

"Cool!" said Nep, grinning at the possibilities.

"Believe I, it can be mostings annoysome," said the globbatrotter.

"I wonder what Pythagoras usually says?" said Nep.

"Oh, he be swearing all the time," said Merlin. "Grumpy old prickle-claw!"

"I hope he's okay," said Nep. "I hope Morgan le Fay hasn't hurt him... What's that?" Nep had noticed a faint green light flashing in the distance.

"That be just a littling glow-worm," said Merlin. "It be a female flashing her light to attract a male. Though, actually, they be not worms at all; they be beetles. I be having no idea why you human beans do be calling them worms. In King Arthur's day, worms be dragons, which be another fishy kettle altogether!"

"Merlin," said Nep, "do you think Morgan le Fay is still here? She scares me."

"I be not sure," said the globbatrotter. "She scarifies me too. She seemed to vanish soon after she did attackle poor Mistress Otter. That were mostings dreadful." Merlin's long ears flopped down sadly. "And her with young'uns an' all."

They both sat in silence as they recalled the terrible attack.

"Where do you think the sorceress went?" asked Nep at last.

"Perhaps she did be returning to your prickle-claw? Morgan le Fay seems to be requiring the bodies of human beans and creatures to be hiding within."

"I'm so worried about Pythagoras," said Nep. "He's grumpy but I do love him."

"I knows you does," said Merlin softly.

After a pause, Nep asked, "What do you think the sorceress will do with us?"

"Now that be something I be not liking to consider. I mostings certainly do not wish to be possessed by devilish evil and thickly smoke. After all, smoking be very bad for you."

"Merlin?" whispered Nep, peering around to make sure the toads were still sleeping.

"Yeah?"

"What's that rhyme all about? The one she keeps saying that we mustn't repeat. What does she mean when she says 'when the names are in place' and the story retold'?"

"Ah, that be the crux of the whole matter, methinks. That be why all this unfortunate business be occurring."

Lowering his voice, the globbatrotter told Nep about King Arthur who had lived many centuries ago, and Merlin the First who had been his court magician. Nep still didn't believe that Merlin, the legendary wizard, could possibly have been a little globbatrotter, but he let his friend continue with his tale.

Apparently, when King Arthur's half-sister, the sorceress Morgan le Fay, had died, her final words had been the curse that Nep had now heard twice. Perhaps Morgan le Fay had predicted that the names of her family would be used once again in the future – allowing her to return, to wreak havoc on the world.

"So, which names are in place?" asked Nep, still puzzling over the rhyme.

The globbatrotter reminded him that his father's real name was Robert Arthur Pendragon Trout; he just preferred to be called Bob for short. Bob's sister, having a very similar name to the sorceress, was Morgana Faye. Apparently, Bob's father had been a lover of Arthurian legend and couldn't resist giving his children these unusual names.

"But what about Guinevere?" asked Nep. "Who's she?"

"That be your dear, departed mother," said the globbatrotter gently. "The mostings loving and kind human bean to grace this earth, according to your father."

"But Dad said her name was Gwen."

"And what do you think Gwen be short for?" said Merlin.

"Oh... I see."

It had seemed like an incredible coincidence when Bob had met his true love, Guinevere. After all, not many girls were given that medieval name these days. But Bob's father had been overjoyed to think that the historic names were once again in place.

"Of coursings, all would have been well, if you hadn't come along," said Merlin.

"Thanks."

"You sees, Bob and Gwen did raise you from 'a babe to a child', as predicted – and the curse of the sorceress could then be coming true."

"But why would she care if Mum and Dad had a child?" asked Nep. "What does it matter to her? We're not even related to King Arthur; the names are just a coincidence."

"I knows. But I think Morgan le Fay always be the jealous, bitter kind. She never be having a family of her own, you sees, and I do not think she could be bearing it. You are something she never had."

"I wonder what she plans to do."

Merlin thought for a moment.

"Cause misery and chaos?" he suggested. "World domination perhaps?" They noticed another glow-worm flashing in the distance. "Or perhaps she be after you, Neptune, so that she can call you her own?"

Nep shivered.

★

After a long and bumpy bus ride on roads flooded by heavy rains, Bob had arrived in the pretty village of Jiri, nestled in the hills of rural Nepal. This was as far as he could go by road. From here, it would be about two weeks' trek on foot to Mount Everest.

But Bob knew the route well, and he relished every step of it – despite it being the height of monsoon season. He had waterproof clothing with him, thanks to Nep, and he'd never minded the rain. Also, this was a less popular time of year to travel to Everest, so he would hopefully be able to explore much of the countryside in peace and quiet.

Every part of the journey was full of wonder. Bob enjoyed waiting beside narrow bridges for yaks to cross; their long horns had been known to gouge people, so he always kept still and waited patiently for the large animals to pass. He loved pausing at Mani stones. These stones were often built into lengths of wall that divided the path. The walls displayed Tibetan Buddhist mantras, and sometimes they contained prayer wheels too. Bob knew to always walk to the left of the Mani walls, circling them in a clockwise direction – to show his respect for the Buddhist faith – and he would spin the prayer wheels and say a prayer each time.

From green, leafy Jiri, he planned to walk to Bhandar with its wonderful white shrine. There were always plenty of Tibetan shrinking toadstools to pick in this area, if they hadn't been washed away by the rain. Next, he'd pass through the terraced village of Sete, and then Junbesi with its imposing monastery. After that, he'd cross a few rivers on rickety bridges to reach Nuntala, high in the hills, where he'd stop to buy more supplies. He also hoped to find some lamsinpoo and itchicara tree bark here. The village of Buhpsa would offer another gleaming white shrine, fluttering prayer flags and a Buddhist monastery. Every village was breathtakingly beautiful. And all the while, he'd be looking out for any other rare plants he could find.

As the altitude increased and his breathing became more strained, Bob would arrive in the settlement of Ghat with its large stone houses that wound their way up the hill. Just before Namche Bazaar, he would pass the hair-raising runway at Lukla, which was frighteningly steep, and he would realise with some nervousness that he would be taking off from this small airport on his return journey.

From the terraces of Namche Bazaar, cut into the sheer hillside, he would at last be able to see several towering, mist-shrouded peaks. His final destination would be Everest Base Camp, almost 37 kilometres from Namche Bazaar. He couldn't wait to see it again!

No one could contact him here; he was completely alone. But he felt peaceful and at one with nature. How he loved being alive and free.

★

Poor Margot was worn out. Each night, for almost a week, she'd roamed the Avalon Marshes. At dawn, she'd return to the farm to carry out her sheepdog duties, only to set out at dusk to search again.

Lord Swan had explained that the army of toads, along with the globbatrotter and small boy, were on the other side of the River Brue, somewhere near the village of Godney. But Margot had never been that far from home before and the territory was new to her.

Frantically, using her powerful sense of smell, she'd search each field and ditch, trying to catch a whiff of boy or globbatrotter. But every night there would be distractions too: the beguiling aroma of sheep poo, for example, or cow dung, or rabbits, or mysterious low-flying bats, or sleeping river birds – and once the glorious scent of sausages cooking on a fisherman's camping stove. Irresistible! And always, wherever she went, the strong scent of peat. It was very easy to forget one's mission altogether.

The days and nights were passing by and she wondered if she'd ever find Merlin and Neptune. Would they even be alive by now?

Margot also couldn't locate Lord Swan, who had gone in search of the body of Mistress Otter. The creatures of fur and feather had become separated; the plan had gone wrong.

PART 3

CHAPTER 1: ENOUGH IS ENOUGH

"I be not drinking any more putrid marsh water, and I be not eating any more crickets, flies, snails nor worms!" shouted Merlin the Globbatrotter, stamping his feet. "They be mostings disgusting! If you would only untie us, Neptune and I could be eating some deliciousness what is cheese and crackers right here inside my very own bag – food to which we be mostings partial. I could even be letting you try a crumb or two, if you so wished..."

Unimpressed by the globbatrotter's outburst, the expressionless toad guzzled all of the worms and insects himself then crawled over the marshy humps and tussocks back to the rest of the battalion.

"I didn't think he'd fall for it," whispered Nep.

"I be not understanding," muttered Merlin. "Toads have 'not so much brain as ear-wax'[8]. I thought that brute would be falling for my trick."

Nep sighed deeply. "They'll never let us go, Merlin. It's hopeless. I think they want us to rot here."

The braided-grass ropes were tied so tightly around their hands and feet that they could barely feel their fingers and toes. The two friends huddled together on the ground, feeling miserable and dejected.

"Oh, oh, oh!" wailed Merlin suddenly, making Nep jump out of his skin. "I feel such terrible fainting and dizzying spells overcoming I. I must be needing a doctor mostings urgently – or a learned person who do be knowing about worts and herbal medicines... like Bob, for example, who do be living back in the village–"

"But he's gone to–" blurted Nep.

"Sssshhh!" hissed Merlin. "They do not be knowing that." Then in a louder voice, he continued, "Oh dear, oh dear. I am afeared I may be breathing my very last breath. I is gasping, gasping. Helps I, please!" He coughed and flailed about dramatically.

The toads just sighed. It was nearly two weeks since they'd captured the tiny boy and the pig-like creature, and the two of them had done nothing but complain. The toads rested their heads on the damp grass and soon the whole army was snoozing again.

Nep and Merlin couldn't understand why they were being kept at the toads' base for so long. After all, they hadn't seen the sorceress in ages. What on earth was going on?

"Well, I do be reckoning enough is enough," whispered the globbatrotter. "I believe the time has come."

"For what?" asked Nep, shuffling closer.

"For magick, that's what!" said the globbatrotter. "Bob always be a-telling I that I must not be doing my spells in public, in case they do be drawing attention to myself. But I do believe this unfortunate situation may now be deemed an emergency."

"What? It's taken you thirteen days to decide that?!" said Nep, exasperated.

"Yeah, well, I have been pondering it for many a day outs and ins, and I do believe I have reached the correct and proper decision. While those warty devils do be sleeping, I will try to release our bonds.

The only problem is, I be not very good at doing magick quietly. I might be needing you to sing, Neptune."

"Sing?"

"Yeah, to be covering up my mostings mighty and impressive casting-spells voice."

"Are you serious? All the toads will wake up."

"Those roly-poly jelly-bellies be not caring if you sings for a while, Nep. They be mostings uncultured. Sing some opera, that be about the right volume."

"Opera? I don't know any opera. Dad only plays songs from the sixties."

"Could you not be making something up – something of a wailing, moaning, outpouring nature?"

"No, I couldn't."

"Oh…"

The two friends eventually agreed to wait for nightfall when the toads would wake up naturally and wander off in search of food.

★

The steppe eagle, known as a 'booted eagle' because of her fluffy, feathery legs, usually spent her days sailing gracefully over the red cliffs and columns of the Charyn Canyon.

This particular eagle had been brave to accept the mission from the white stork. So many of her kind had been lost in recent years, due to increasing wildfires and vicious pests that would attack their nests; the warming climate had a lot to answer for. But, four days ago, when the Ukrainian stork had asked her to take her turn in the Ancient Sky Journey, she knew she had no choice but to help. As the national bird of Kazakhstan, even appearing on the country's flag, she was a proud bird – not one to decline a daring quest! Now, the strong, brown eagle glided southwards, away from the Almaty Region, rising effortlessly on warm currents of air, barely needing to flap her long wings as she flew. Travelling at fifty miles per hour, Pakistan was almost in sight.

CHAPTER 2: STINKY CHEESE AND SOGGY CRACKERS

Except for the click and hum of insects, the night-time marshes were quiet and still. The toads had left their two prisoners alone under the willow tree, to go hunting after dark.

"So much for the frogs turning up then," muttered Merlin to himself. "Unreliable creatures. They all be dickie in the noddle, if you asks me. Well, I be having quite enough of this caper." He sat up and nudged Nep. "Time for spells, Neptune!"

Startled from a nightmare, Nep woke up with a shriek. For a moment, he couldn't work out where he was.

"There, there, young'un," said Merlin reassuringly. "You did be having that upsettifying dream of yours again."

Nep breathed deeply and tried to calm his racing heart.

"I just don't get it," he said, feeling flustered. "It's not Aunt Morgana in my dream, it's someone else. A younger woman. She's really pretty, with long hair. But she's surrounded by smoke, just like my aunt was on the landing. And there's something else..." Nep paused, unable to continue.

"You can tell I, young sir," said the globbatrotter gently.

"She's reaching out towards me. She can't quite get hold of my hand. I think she wants me to save her. But I can't, Merlin. I can't. And I don't know why. She's so scared and I can't do anything to help her."

"I be's not knowing why, Neptune. I really be's not knowing... Now, listen, if you can be gathering yourself somewhats, we will be trying to leave this damp patch of toadiness. It is time for us to be wells and trulies on our way."

Leaning all of his weight against the willow tree behind him, Merlin braced his legs and slowly pushed himself up to a standing position. Then, steadying himself against the tree trunk, he closed his eyes in concentration and loudly pronounced:

"Good battles evil,
light destroys the night,
peace will overcome
the hate and the fight.

When help is required,
magick will reply,
when the foxes bark
and the owls do cry.

Then bonds will shatter
and all will be free,
as Merlin foretold
at Glastonbury."

Nep held his breath and waited. The warm night air seemed to hold its breath too. But nothing happened. Then, far in the distance, Nep heard a fox bark and an owl hoot at almost the same moment. Instantly, the plaited-grass ropes loosened around their wrists and ankles and slid to the ground.

"Wow!" gasped Nep, in awe. "I'm going to memorise that spell. It's amazing!" He shook his hands and feet to try to bring them back to life. "You really did that, didn't you?"

"Of coursings I did, you cabbage-head!"

"So, you really are descended from Merlin the First?"

"Yeah."

"I mean, from King Arthur's very own magician?"

"Yeah."

"And Merlin the First really was a globbatrotter?"

Merlin the Eighth sighed. "Of coursings he were. I have told you that beforewhiles."

"Wow!" said Nep, clambering to his feet, his eyes and mouth still gaping.

"Well, is you to be coming with I to escape, or is you to be standing there likes a vacant golding fish?" asked Merlin.

"I be coming with you to escape," said Nep absently. "Um, I mean.... yeah, good idea. Let's go."

Twinkling in the dark sky, there were just enough stars for Merlin to navigate by. He turned his crinkly snout upwards and studied them for some time.

"Yeah, they did be bringing us some ways north, I reckons," said the globbatrotter, peering at the North Star through his thick glasses.

"Oh no, that means we've got even further to go," moaned Nep.

"Never minds, Neptune. If we can be a-keeping that twinkle-star known as Polaris behind us, we will be retracing our steps. We can cross a bridge what human beans does use to be saving us some time."

"Are you sure that's Polaris?"

"Oh yeah. Polaris be the North Star – the only bright star whose place do not be changing in the sky, other than to be going somewhats higher or lower."

"If you say so."

"I do be saying so. We globbatrotters be both wizards and navigators, remember. Now, we must be travelling south to the river post-haste. As William Shakespeare hisself do say, 'Once more unto the bridge, dear friend'[9]!"

Merlin set off at a steady trot and Nep did his best to keep up, but the ground was lumpy and slippery and he kept falling over. Also, he'd eaten nothing but dandelion leaves for two weeks and he felt weak and tired. But after half an hour's determined plodding, they reached a channel known as the Division Rhyne and stopped at its edge. There was no bridge in sight.

"How will we get to Glastonbury now?" said Nep, close to tears. "Swan has disappeared. The Quacking Nancy's miles away. Heron's flying to

London. Poor Otter's dead. It's impossible, Merlin. It's the end of the road."

"No, I think you will be finding this is a river," said the globbatrotter, peering down.

Nep burst into tears and sank to the ground, weeping.

"Oh dear, oh dear, young'un. Look, I still be having my bag with me. Let us stop for a few moments and taste some of this toothsome cheese. And these crackers what have lost most of their crack. I think the plums be rather squashed, a littling mouldy and perhaps somewhats smelly. But the cheese be mature and full of ripe deliciousness."

He passed some food to Nep, who ate the stinky cheese and soggy crackers hungrily.

"I believe I even be having a small bottle of my homemade elderflower cordial here," smiled the globbatrotter, reaching into his bag with his stubby fingers. "Please do be having it. I can slurp on dirty rhyne water, but that not be healthy for human personages."

Nep drank all of the juice in seconds and then ate some more cheese.

"Oh, that's better," he said. "Thank you, Merlin. Thank you for looking after me."

"*Ah, there you are!*" came a loud voice from behind them.

They both spun round, terrified.

"I've been searching the marshes for you, night after night. Where *have* you been?" It was a panting, wagging, bright-eyed Margot.

"Oh, Margot!" cried Nep, jumping up and throwing his arms around her furry leg.

"Well, I must be admitting, I be feeling mostings pleased to see you, Miss Margot," said

Merlin. "And relieved. And I never thought I, a globbatrotter, would be saying that about a dog."

Margot tipped her head on one side, looking slightly offended.

"But I be meaning that mostings respectfully," said Merlin with a bow.

"How did you find us?" asked Nep, gazing up at her shining black nose and lolling pink tongue.

"Well, I smelt strong cheese and fermenting plums, didn't I?" she said. "Yes, I did. I did indeed." Her nose was working overtime. "Do you have a little to spare, perhaps? Of the cheese, I mean. It seems to be matured to perfection."

The globbatrotter put a few small pieces on the ground for her to eat.

"Mmmm, lovely," grinned the collie. "My favourite! Well, actually, I think sausages are my favourite. Though bacon comes a close second. And a juicy bone from the butcher's shop is most appetising." Her nose sniffed around Merlin's bag. "Do I detect crackers as well?"

The globbatrotter laughed and passed her some damp crumbs.

"Can you help us, please?" said Nep.

"Why, of course," said Margot. "Anything at all. Just say the word. Though I must be back by morning. I must round up the sheep, nip the cows, lick the children–"

"Yes, yes, we be knowing all that," said Merlin.

"Quite so. Do forgive me," said Margot, lying down beside them in the grass, her tail still wagging.

"Have you seen Swan?" asked Nep. "And is Heron back yet?"

"It was Lord Swan who sent me to find you," said Margot. "But the search has been harder than I thought it would be. So many distractions, you see – what with the bats, and the sausages, and the peat, and the poo–"

"Is he okay?" asked Nep.

"Who?"

"Lord Swan."

"Oh yes, he's very well, thank you. Very well indeed. He thought I might be able to sneak into the toads' camp, you see. But, as I say, it's been a complex mission – what with the peat and the–"

"And Heron?" asked Nep.

"No sign of Sir Heron yet, I'm afraid," said Margot.

"Oh dear, I do be hoping he is keeping safies and soundies," said Merlin.

"Still, at least Mistress Otter is back with her cubs," said Margot.

"What?!" cried Nep and Merlin together.

"I said, at least Mistress Otter–"

"We know what you did be saying, Miss Margot," said the globbatrotter. "But we cannot be believing it. We did be thinking poor Mistress Otter were deadified."

"Ah, well, she was in pretty bad shape. We think she's broken a couple of ribs. And she had a terrible headache that lasted a week. And she was suffering from shock, of course. She won't be travelling far for a while, but she's suckling her cubs and Lord Swan is catching fish and eels for her to eat. They're quite a partnership, you know. Though he won't be able to leave her side for some time."

"Yes, of coursings," nodded Merlin.

"Oh, I'm so happy!" cried Nep, overcome with relief. "I really thought she'd died trying to save us."

"Indeedy, yes," smiled Merlin. "Good, brave, kind Mistress Otter. The finest otter in the whole of Avalon."

"I agree," said Nep.

"Well, now I've found you, and we've had a lovely chat, I suppose I'd better be going. Thanks for the cheese! I'll report back to Lord Swan," said the sheepdog, getting up. "He'll be so pleased when I tell him I've located you. He certainly will – of that, I'm sure."

"Miss Margot?" said Merlin. "Before you dash off..."

"Yes?"

"Do you think it would be possible for you to be mostings kindly carrying Neptune and I upon your strong back? I be's sure you will be able to find your way back to the River Brue, and perhaps even further beyond, and it will be making the journey so much easier for us personages what is somewhats smaller than yourself."

"Why, yes, it will be an absolute pleasure. The honour will be all mine. What a privilege it will be."

"Thank you," smiled Nep.

Margot lay down on the ground and rolled onto her side so that Merlin and Nep could crawl over her ribcage and up onto her thickly coated neck. Then she carefully stood up again.

"Holding tight?" she asked.

Merlin slung his bag over his shoulder and wrapped some of Margot's long black hairs around his hands.

"Get a good grip, little'un," Merlin said to Nep, who was sitting in front of him.

"Okay, ready," said Nep.

"Right, here we go!" said the enthusiastic dog, taking a few steps back then charging, full tilt, at the wide stream.

"Oh no! She be going to jump!" cried Merlin.

"Aaaaaaaaagghhh!" screamed Nep.

Merlin and Nep shut their eyes as the sheepdog leapt athletically across the water. Time seemed to stand still as she sailed through the air above the rhyne. Then with a great jolt, she hit the ground running.

Nep and Merlin had never had such a bumpy ride over the marshes in all their lives – and Merlin's life had been very long.

"This must be like riding on an elephant on a pogo stick!" said Nep, his teeth banging together and his whole body shuddering.

"He be shaking my bones out of my garments,"[10] said the globbatrotter. "And my brain be more fuddled even than usuals."

The three friends streaked through the blackness of Avalon, completely unseen by toads or humans. But, of course, Morgan le Fay wasn't human...

CHAPTER 3: CHOMOLUNGMA

Bob had made good time and, at last, breathing hard due to the altitude, he was approaching Everest's South Base Camp. At this height of 5,364 metres above sea level, he didn't need to use an oxygen cylinder, but breathing was still difficult. He realised that the long days he'd spent in the lab hadn't helped his fitness; his leg muscles were burning and his back was aching due to the strain of carrying his heavy rucksack.

Despite still being below the snowline, it was incredibly cold for the time of year. If the wind picked up any more, he thought he might turn blue. But, as he looked around him, he couldn't believe how many people were passing him, climbing both up and down the mountain. It seemed that since his last visit to Nepal, scaling the highest peak in the world had become big business.

On reaching the many tents of Base Camp, though, his heart sank and he nearly burst into tears. He couldn't believe it! Litter was strewn far across the barren, windswept ground. People had abandoned their tents, equipment and rubbish. Plastic bags, boxes and bottles lay everywhere. His beloved mountain had become a trash heap. He simply couldn't take it in. He knew that for Hindus and Buddhists, the mountain had great spiritual significance. Indeed, the Tibetan name for Everest was Chomolungma, which means 'Mother Goddess of the World'. How could anyone have done this to the Mother Goddess?

Not only that, but it was rumoured that the South Base Camp would soon have to be moved to a new location at a lower altitude because it was becoming too dangerous to camp by the Khumbu Glacier. Global warming was melting the ice, making it thin and unstable. What were humankind doing to this beautiful place, and to the world?

Bob made an instant decision to take another route. He wasn't planning on climbing any higher, so he would explore the surrounding area on his own, away from the clutter and mess. With mighty, snow-covered Everest looming over him, he carefully picked his way across the rocky moonscape and headed towards a distant ravine.

Though he knew there would be safety in numbers, there would be peace in solitude. He would opt for peace.

★

Jesh and Mary couldn't understand what had happened to their friend Ned. They hadn't seen him in days. They knew his posh aunt had arrived, but they hadn't spotted her, Ned or Bob since then; they'd simply vanished. Even the sulky cat had gone missing.

Several times, they'd knocked on Ned's front door to ask if he'd like to come out to play football, but there had never been a reply.

"Maybe they've gone on holiday," suggested Mary, as they wandered back down the road.

"Don't you think he'd have told us?" said Jesh.

"Maybe he's gone to live with his aunt."

"Poor Ned!"

"Or maybe he's embarrassed to see us now that we know his real name," said Mary.

"I hope not," said Jesh. "I miss him. Anyway, it doesn't matter what he's called; he's our friend."

"Exactly," said Mary. "I've got a weird middle name. I've never told anyone what it is."

"Well, what is it?" asked Jesh.

"Promise you won't tell?"

"Of course."

"Go on, say it..." said Mary.

"I promise I won't tell. Cross my heart."

"It's Grimonia. I was named after my great-grandmother, who was named after a saint."

"Mary Grimonia Kelly?"

"That's me."

"I like it," smiled Jesh.

"Really? I hate it. But wait till I tell Ned – I mean, Neptune. He won't feel half as bad!"

Jesh laughed.

"Perhaps we should put a note through his door to say we'd like to see him," said Mary. "Do you think that would help?"

"That's a great idea," said Jesh. "We could tell him we miss him."

They both hurried back to Mary's house to find a piece of paper and a pen.

CHAPTER 4: THE SORCERESS RETURNS

Bumping up and down on Margot's back, Nep and Merlin admired the first rays of dawn glinting on the dew-covered fields. The distant sound of birdsong grew in volume to become a full-blown and glorious chorus.

"What a beautiful place this be," said Merlin, his voice shaky from all the bouncing. "And I be having the good company of friends now too. Though I do be missing my globbatrotter family mostings terribly, the friendlyships I have made with you, Neptune, and my fur-and-feather companions, they do be bringing a sense of love and contentedness to my heart."

"Me too," smiled Nep. "I'm so glad I met you, Merlin the Globbatrotter."

"Sorry about the bumpy ride," panted Margot, covering the distance as quickly as she could.

"Be not worried, my friend," said Merlin. "As the Bard hisself do say, 'The course of true love never did run smooth'[11]."

"I'm afraid I'll have to leave you soon," said the sheepdog as she trotted beside the River Brue, following it south towards Wearyall Hill. "I simply mustn't be late back to the farm. I have so many responsibilities. Have I told you about them?"

"Yes, you have," said Nep, cutting her off. "Several times."

"If you could just be getting us to the edge of Glastonbury, we would be mostings grateful, Miss Margot," said the globbatrotter. "I can see the Tor clearly now. I feel sure it be only a mile away if that."

"Very well, but we'll have to hurry," said Margot, breaking into a run, as Nep and Merlin clung onto her fur.

"Merlin, you *did* say there's an antidote, didn't you, to make me big again?" said Nep, his whole body juddering.

"Oh yeah, don't you be worrying about that, young sir," said the globbatrotter, his voice trembling as much as his belly. "There definitely be a wort to be reversing the shrinking. The only place it do grow be the Isle of Avalon – or Glastonbury Tor, as you knows it. The plant be called sword-in-the-stone."

"You're joking!" laughed Nep.

"No."

"You have *got* to be kidding me."

"No, I be mostings serious. It be a tiny plant, with a long straight stem what do resemble a sword. Its little flowers be silvery grey."

"Well, I never," said Nep. "Will it be easy to find?"

"Well, although it be small, and the only plant of its kind known to human beans or globbatrotters, I feel sure I will be sniffing it out with my impressive hooter," said Merlin. "The difficulty will be in picking it," he added.

"Why's that?" asked Nep, his voice still shuddering.

"Well, its roots grow so deeply into the earth that it be almost impossible to be pulling it out of the ground."

"Can't I just take some of its leaves or petals?" asked Nep.

"No, it be the roots what you do be needing. They be making a foul-tasting tea, I do believe, when brewed in boiling water. Or you can be chewing them raw. That is what will be unshrinking you."

"But how are we going to pull it out of the ground?"

"I be having no ideas at all," said the globbatrotter, his teeth clanging in his large, orange head. "All we can be doing is hoping. And not just for your sakes either."

"What do you mean?"

"Well, my ancestors did be telling I that the only way to be stopping the sorceress, Morgan le Fay, from returning in different ghostly guises over multitudinous years would be to be removing the sword-in-the-stone from the ground once and for all. That be the only way to be stopping her vile and evil ways."

"No pressure then," said Nep.

★

Beside the long, straight river, not far from Meare, Mistress Otter lay in a deep burrow under a rotting tree stump. Her cracked ribs and bruised head were still sore, but she was healing well. Only yesterday, she'd thanked Lord Swan and told him she'd be able to catch her own fish and eels now. Then he could go in search of their missing friends.

Snuggled up to the otter's warm belly were two small cubs. When she'd first given birth to them, they'd been blind and helpless, but now their jet-black, twinkling eyes gazed up at her lovingly. Her heart filled with pride and affection, just knowing that her little ones were safe and well, and that she'd managed to get back to the holt to care for them.

For now, she'd spend eight hours a day nursing them. But soon, when the cubs were just over ten weeks old, Mistress Otter would lead them out of their cosy home for the first time. What an adventure it would be!

In all, her youngsters would stay with her for a year. During that time, she would guard them fiercely. She would risk her life for them, if she had to – just as she'd risked her life for her friends Neptune and Merlin. She still wondered what had happened to the tiny boy and the globbatrotter. Had they even survived?

As Mistress Otter poked her head out of her den, a huge bird skimmed over the water. She noted how slow and laboured its wingbeats were. The old heron looked drained.

"Oh, he's made it back! Thank goodness!" she sighed. Then, turning to her cubs, she said, "That's Sir Heron, little ones. You'll meet him one day. He's the noblest and wisest bird in the whole of Somerset."

★

As Margot approached Wearyall Hill, its hawthorn tree silhouetted against the dawn, she and her two passengers noticed something moving on the western slopes. It was a four-legged something – graceful and large.

"What's that?" said Nep, pointing.

"Methinks it do be having a long tail," said Merlin, squinting through his thick lenses. "It be looking very much like a prickle-claw to me."

Margot came to a halt and sniffed the air.

"Definitely a cat, in my opinion," she said. "But is it my eyesight, or is it much bigger than it should be?"

Nep gasped.

"You're right, it's absolutely huge! Dad's told me about big cats roaming around Somerset – escaped panthers and things like that. But I never thought I'd ever see one."

The amber eyes of the large brown cat focused on them, unblinking.

"It looks just like a puma," said Nep, thinking back to his animal encyclopaedia. "Do you think it's a puma, Merlin?"

"I never be seeing a puma before, so I cannot be saying," said the globbatrotter. "But it be looking mostings unfriendly – nay, it be looking dangerous."

Slowly, on soft paws, the cat descended the green slope and strolled towards them.

"No!" cried Nep, suddenly afraid. "No, it can't be!"

"What?" said Merlin, clutching onto Nep.

"It's Pythagoras. But he's massive... puma-sized."

"What do we do?" asked a panic-stricken Margot.

The globbatrotter, obviously shaken, said nothing.

"Merlin? Merlin?" said Nep. "What do we do?"

"That explains where she did be all those days outs and ins," he said at last.

"Who? Morgan le Fay?"

"Yeah, she be gaining in strength and cunning. She be growing into a mighty force for evil. There be no stopping her now."

"Shall I run?" asked Margot, her ears back and her tail between her legs.

"DO YOU HONESTLY THINK YOU CAN RUN FROM ME?" came a booming voice from the huge cat, though its mouth didn't move. "YOU STAND NO CHANCE, YOU PATHETIC CREATURE."

Margot began to tremble.

"Oh dear, oh dear," she whined.

As the cat drew closer, its yellow eyes changed to a hypnotic blue and, with a loud *whoosh*, thick grey smoke rushed up from its body in a massive, billowing cloud.

Merlin's voice was quaking.

"Oh no, she be mighty powerful. She be going to kill us."

"THAT'S RIGHT, OF COURSE I'M GOING TO KILL YOU, YOU RIDICULOUS BEAST. JUST AS I KILLED GUINEVERE."

Neptune's face turned pale.

"Guinevere?" he said. "My mother? Did you kill my mother?"

The cloud quickly formed into a gigantic mushroom shape, as if an atomic bomb had just exploded on the Somerset Levels. The height of a skyscraper, it filled the air above the emerald fields.

"DON'T YOU REMEMBER, NEPTUNE?" cackled the thunderous voice.

As they watched, the mist swirled and twisted, transforming into the shape of a tall woman in a long gown – only this time her outline was much more solid.

"YOU WERE VERY YOUNG AT THE TIME, BUT HOW YOU WEPT! YOU CRIED AND CRIED." Again, monstrous laughter erupted. "SURELY, YOU REMEMBER THAT?"

"My dream," whispered Nep, grabbing hold of Merlin's arm. "The woman in my dream was my mother." Tears flowed down his ashen face. "Morgan le Fay killed my mother, and I was there," he sobbed.

"I be so very sorry," said Merlin, hugging the boy. "My heart, it be breaking for you."

But Neptune's heart was bursting with an intense and raging anger.

"*I hate you!*" he screamed at the cloud sorceress. "*I hate you!* My mum begged me to save her, but I couldn't. You took her away from me!"

"YOUR MOTHER WASN'T BEGGING YOU TO SAVE HER," laughed Morgan le Fay, her hollow eyes fixed on Neptune. "DON'T BE SO FOOLISH. YOU WERE MERELY AN INFANT. HOW COULD YOU POSSIBLY HAVE SAVED YOUR MOTHER? SHE WAS PUSHING YOU AWAY; SHE WAS TRYING TO SAVE YOU FROM ME, YOU STUPID CHILD. IN FACT, SHE DID SAVE YOU. BUT YOU HAVE ALWAYS BEEN MY TARGET, NEPTUNE, SON OF ARTHUR, AND NOW I'M BACK FOR YOU!"

"*I hate you!*" screamed Nep, shaking uncontrollably. "*I hate–*"

But he didn't have time to finish his sentence because Margot, in a panic, was on the run. Like a sleek, black arrow, she raced away from the deadly smog towards the river.

"Hold on!" she said as she leapt headlong into the River Brue, plunging into the water with a great splash.

Still clutching onto her back, Merlin and Nep were completely submerged. Holding their breath, they tried frantically to climb up Margot's neck and out of the water.

Nep managed to get his head above water first.

"Hold on!" he spluttered, struggling to pull Merlin up behind him.

"I be holding on!" coughed the globbatrotter as his face eventually appeared. "And I not be letting go."

Then, without warning, silent toads appeared on the riverbanks. The amphibians were everywhere!

"Not again," cried Nep, remembering what had happened to Lord Swan.

The ugly creatures slid into the river and swam awkwardly towards Margot. And all the while, Morgan le Fay's evil laughter cracked the air.

Nep tried once more to drag Merlin out of the water, but he was a dead weight. The two friends were losing their grip on Margot's wet fur and, to make matters worse, toads were now scrabbling at the dog's back. There were so many of them!

"Jealousy, you monster, you shall be paying for this!" gargled the globbatrotter, scowling at the green-eyed toad on the bank. "When I get hold of you, I shall be letting out your puddings!"

Poor Margot couldn't bear the weight of so many toads on her back; she was in danger of sinking. Frantically, she thrashed about, trying to keep afloat.

"Help me! Help me!" she whimpered.

But then, ranks and ranks of brown speckled frogs were hopping out of the grass and plopping into the water. There were legions of them – so many, they made the water seem solid. Some drifted up from the riverbed, their bulbous eyes appearing beside the flailing dog.

"At last! Where in goodness graciousness have you been?!" gasped Merlin, taking a breath before he disappeared underwater again, along with the toad-encrusted collie and Nep, who was hanging onto Margot's ear.

Kicking their long, powerful legs, the frogs glided easily through the water. Luckily, they were strong swimmers and they had another weapon that the toads lacked – teeth! Diving down, they grabbed hold of the toads' legs and bit them mercilessly.

Meanwhile, on the bank, several frogs leapt onto Jealousy in a 'flying body press' wrestling move and pinned him to the ground, where he struggled and kicked angrily. Other frogs wrestled escaping toads, using the 'diving chop', 'frog splash' and other aerial tactics. Flattened toads lay everywhere, winded and groaning.

In the water, injured toads were floating up to the surface and trying to squeeze between the soup of frogs. But the toads were quickly pursued by their agile enemy, who vaulted onto them in an effort to sink them again. Though larger and heavier, the toads were simply outnumbered and outmanoeuvred.

As battle-weary toads clambered onto the bank and limped away, a frantic, puffing Margot appeared above the surface again, with a sopping globbatrotter and small boy still attached to her fur. A few of the frogs scrambled onto Margot's back and tried to shove Merlin up onto the dog's head, where he would be safely out of the water.

But the cloud sorceress was furious; she was spinning like a twister in the Great Plains of America. She whirled round and round at a frantic speed until she was a dangerous tornado approaching the river.

"She will be drowning us," cried the globbatrotter. "I be no swimmer. You must be saving yourselves."

The frogs leapt off Margot and plummeted into the depths, while others abandoned the fight and disappeared into the reeds. As the remaining frogs – a squirming mass of glossy bodies – tried to reach the riverside, the water spun and churned around them, dragging them down in a deadly spiral. Soon the whole river was spinning, and the three friends were being sucked down inside a terrifying whirlpool. As the sorceress twisted wildly above them, there seemed to be no escape. And though Margot fought bravely to reach the surface, her lungs ached and she knew she was going to drown.

But the whirling vortex of water suddenly lifted the three of them up, carrying them out of the river and up into the air. An exhausted Margot struggled and whined, but she was powerless in the sorceress's grasp.

"Take I!" yelled the globbatrotter. "Take I and be letting the boy and dog go! Let the boy go home to his father, I be begging you."

As the whirlpool finally slowed down and released them, the three friends fell to the grass with a thud. The river water fell too, drenching the already soaked trio as, worn out and dizzy, they lay helplessly beneath the coiling, reforming mist.

"WHAT A NOBLE GESTURE FOR A PREPOSTEROUS LITTLE PIG!" seethed Morgan le Fay as her hazy form convulsed above them. "HOW VERY BRAVE YOU ARE!" Her voice was crazy and thundering. "WHY WOULD I WANT YOU, YOU BRAINLESS BEAST? IT IS THE BOY I WANT! IT IS THE BOY I HAVE WANTED ALL ALONG. HE WILL BE MINE! I SHALL MAKE HIM POWERFUL AND MIGHTY LIKE ME. I WILL TEACH HIM EVERYTHING I KNOW OF THE DARK WAYS. HE WILL BE MY VERY OWN SON AND HEIR."

"*We're not even related!*" screamed Nep, horrified. "*The names are just a coincidence! None of this makes sense.*"

"WHEN THE NAMES ARE IN PLACE! WHEN THE NAMES ARE IN PLACE!" she roared insanely.

"*Go away!*" cried Nep, overcome with fear. "*Just go away and leave me alone!*"

Out of nowhere, the flapping of large wings sounded above their heads.

"Look!" said Margot, still cowering on the ground. "It's Sir Heron!"

Courageously, the heron flew straight at the dense smoke and pierced a gaping hole in it with his long, sharp beak. But, as he did so, he cried out in pain and several pale feathers fluttered to the ground.

"Careful, Sir Heron," yelled Merlin, "or she will be destroying you!"

"Flee!" cried the old bird, exhausted from his long journey. But that was all he could say before the mist engulfed him.

"Quick, now's our chance," said Margot as she rolled onto her side. "Climb on."

As the heron circled and tried again to attack the cloud sorceress, Nep and Merlin hauled themselves onto Margot's wet back and, in seconds, she was careering across the fields towards Glastonbury.

"Save yourself!" shouted Merlin over his shoulder. "Save yourself, my mostings dear friend."

But Sir Heron had been swallowed by the twining darkness.

CHAPTER 5: IMPOSSIBLE JOURNEYS

Bob had been exploring the rocky ground for most of the afternoon. He knew he only had a short time in Nepal, so he'd been searching intently for the famous Tibetan love flower – in fact, he'd completely lost track of distance and time. Now, the light was dimming and he hadn't even set up camp.

It took a few moments for Bob to notice that he was crunching through snow. Not only that, but snowflakes were falling all around him and the wind was picking up. It looked like a blizzard was on its way. This was strange weather for August; the Mother Goddess must be angry.

Glancing at his gloved hands and mountaineering boots, Bob realised he was so cold he couldn't feel his fingers or toes. He hadn't eaten in hours and he was feeling weak.

Oh, man, he thought. *I'm in trouble!*

He decided to turn around and make his way back to South Base Camp, but he couldn't see anything; the whirling snowflakes had turned into a wall of white. There was no way out of the storm, and if he took a wrong turning, he might fall to his death or end up in a deep crevasse in the glacier, never to be found again.

Bob had made all the mistakes an experienced climber should never make: he hadn't pitched his tent, he hadn't eaten any food, he hadn't told anyone where he was going, he'd lost all sense of direction, and he'd allowed himself to become dangerously cold.

"Man, I'm such an idiot!" he yelled into the blizzard.

Trying not to panic, he used his walking pole to feel his way across the boulder field. Perhaps he could find a nook to climb into, to get out of the blast?

But the wind gusted violently and knocked him off his feet. Lying on the jagged ground, he rubbed his cut head and aching shoulder. Bob suddenly felt out of his depth and afraid. The Mother Goddess deserved respect – even fear; she was fierce and unpredictable. Groaning in pain, he dragged himself up and struggled on.

As quickly as it had come, though, the squall vanished, leaving Bob dazed and bruised, but still in one piece, standing at the edge of the glacier. As daylight was fading fast, he switched on his torch and decided to put up his tent there and then. But, out of the looming darkness, great wings were beating and a huge bird was flying straight at him.

Bob shrieked and ducked down.

"Hey, watch out, goose!"

The beautiful white-headed goose with distinctive black stripes, a dainty beak and a downy grey body almost collided with him. In a commotion of flapping and feathers, the bird landed right beside him and dropped a small, crumpled piece of paper at his feet.

"What in the world...?" said Bob, reaching down to pick up the folded parchment.

He looked from the bird to the paper, mystified. The bird just stared at him, nodded at the message, then flapped its wings and took off into the gloom.

"Hey, goose!" called Bob. "You take care out there, dude."

Shining his torch on the piece of paper, he unwrapped it carefully.

What's going on? thought Bob.

The parchment was so damp and damaged from being carried in so many beaks, and through all kinds of weather, that it was barely readable. The black ink had run down the page and smudged, leaving only three words visible:

"Neptune... danger... hurry!"

Bob scratched his head, trying to comprehend what had just happened. A strange goose had flown up to Everest Base Camp to find him, apparently to give him a message written by someone who knew his son Neptune.

"Globby!" he said out loud. "It must be the globbatrotter. Merlin and Neptune need me!"

There was going to be no time to set up camp, no time to eat or drink, and no time to search for his beloved plants; Bob needed to get home – and fast!

With newfound energy, and a rising sense of panic, he strapped his head torch over his woolly hat and broke into a run. Somehow, he had to find his way back down this huge, scary mountain.

★

Curled in a tight ball beside a hedge, Margot was shaking all over.

"She be not looking too well," said Merlin the Globbatrotter, wringing out his waistcoat.

"I think she's in shock," whispered Nep. "She's been through a lot. She nearly drowned."

"I think we all did be nearly drownding," said the globbatrotter, putting his waistcoat back on and knocking the water out of his furry ears.

Nep knelt down beside the sheepdog.

"Margot?" he said, gently stroking her fur. "Margot, are you okay?"

Margot was moaning in her sleep. She opened one eye briefly then closed it again.

"She be needing to rest, methinks," said Merlin. "She has been bravely getting us as far as Glastonbury, but, poor Missy Margot, she be exhaustipated."

It was the middle of the day and the warm sun was drying them off slowly. Even so, the sheepdog continued to shiver and whine.

"We need to get to the Tor," said Nep, "but we can't leave her here on her own."

"Yes, and the farmer, he will be a-looking for her by nows," said Merlin.

"What did you say?" said Margot, suddenly raising her head and pricking up her ears.

"I did be saying that the farmer, he will be a-looking for you," said the globbatrotter.

"Oh dear, oh dear, I'm late," said Margot, trying to stand up on wobbly legs, but they gave way and she collapsed to the ground.

"You're too weak," said Nep. "You need to rest."

"What you do be needing is some deliciousness what is cheese and crackers," said

Merlin, opening his bag and tipping it upside down. Water poured out of his shoulder bag, along with a mushy heap that once had been food. "Oh dear…"

"Maybe we can find you some food in Glastonbury," said Nep. "Do you think you can walk that far, Margot? We're nearly there now. The road on the other side of this hedge is next to the town. And Tor Hill is just a little bit further. We've almost made it."

Margot shook her head forlornly and shut her eyes.

"What are we going to do?" Nep said, turning to the globbatrotter.

Merlin was still gazing at the sodden remains of their food.

"As Mr William Shakespeare do say, 'We have seen better days'[12]," he said glumly.

"Leave me here," said Margot. "I'm no good to you now. You must finish your quest without me."

"I'm not leaving you," said Nep firmly.

"But when you've swallowed the antidote and grown large again," she said, "you'll be able to help me."

"She do be having a point," said Merlin.

★

Bob's legs were shaky and tired too; he kept falling over as he jogged down the steep, muddy path. It was dark now and the batteries in his head torch were running out. Soon he would have no light at all.

Man, this is such a wipe-out, he thought. *I need to stop* or *I'm going to like totally break my neck.*

He realised he'd have to set up camp, eat and drink something, and try to get some sleep. He'd carry on in the morning when he was more refreshed.

Reaching the runway at Lukla was incredibly urgent, but he'd be no use to Neppy or Merlin the Globbatrotter if he got himself hurt or killed. He would have to be sensible and rest until it was light. Then he would make quicker and safer progress.

★

Far off across the Somerset Levels, a strange indigo cloud was moving north-west, back towards the village of Meare. The size of a hot-air balloon, it glided unnaturally swiftly. While other paler, fluffier clouds drifted with the breeze, heading east, this one was sailing determinedly into the wind.

The cloud left behind a small Burmese cat. Somewhat confused, the cat licked his beautiful brown fur and looked around himself, disorientated. He wondered why that dark, menacing cloud was travelling against the wind, moving so easily in the wrong direction? Wasn't that impossible? Nothing seemed to be as it was. How had he even got here? He had no memory of leaving the house. And where was his family?

As he got up, instinctively knowing the direction of home, he noticed an old heron lying beside the river in a cascade of feathers. There must have been a fight. The bird's grey-white plumage was in disarray and its eyes were closed. It was barely breathing.

But the heron was too large a meal for little Pythagoras. And, anyway, the cat needed to get home. The bird would die soon, and then it would be a meal for the badgers or foxes. It certainly wouldn't go to waste.

★

Feeling small and vulnerable, Nep and Merlin stood beside the bypass in Glastonbury. The road was as wide as two football fields and every few seconds, a huge car would come speeding along it, nearly blowing them over. Each time a gap appeared in the traffic and they thought it would be safe to cross, they had to scuttle back to the kerb – only just reaching it before another car or van hurtled past. Even climbing up the high kerb was incredibly difficult. This plan simply wasn't going to work.

"I thinks we must be waiting for nightfall," puffed Merlin. "Then it will be quieter."

"I hope so," said Nep. "The drivers can't see us, even in daylight. We could be squashed flat."

They crept back to the hedge and crawled through it to find Margot, but the collie had gone.

CHAPTER 6: ICING BUNS

It was lucky that Nadine, a volunteer at Glastonbury's Animal Rescue Centre, was walking her dog by the River Brue that afternoon. Much to her surprise, her Labrador discovered a bedraggled heron lying by the water. At first, the young woman thought the bird was dead – she'd never seen a heron in such a sad and sorry state – but then its chest twitched and one eye flickered.

"Leave it, Clive!" she said, calling her dog away.

She took off her hoodie and gently folded it around the large grey bird.

"We need to get you back to the centre, don't we?" she said, examining the heron's limp body, and the pile of feathers scattered on the ground. "Looks like you've been attacked, poor thing."

Holding the casualty close to her chest, Nadine dashed back to her car with Clive. If she didn't hurry, the bird might die.

As they splashed across the marshy ground, Nadine glanced up at the sky. A large white swan was circling above them, watching their every move.

As the woman put Clive and the heron into the vehicle and drove away, the swan honked furiously, launching himself through the air as fast as he could go. But there was nothing he could do to save Sir Heron.

★

The farmer had searched his fields and sheds all morning for the young black sheepdog. It wasn't like her to disappear – especially at breakfast time. His young children were distraught to learn that Margot was missing from the barn and farmyard. They cried and cried, and couldn't be consoled.

Bringing a couple of sausages with them, which they'd saved from their breakfasts, the farmer and his wife bundled their son and daughter into their pick-up truck and drove down the road, pausing to peer over walls and hedges.

First, they headed towards Westhay, in the Wedmore direction, but there was no sign of a dog anywhere. So, next, they travelled south-east towards Glastonbury. Every once in a while, the husband and wife would climb out of the vehicle to call loudly. The little girl and boy screamed, "*Margot! Margot!*" at the tops of their voices and dangled freshly cooked sausages out of the open windows. But the dog was nowhere to be seen.

"She's never run off before," said the farmer, unaware of the sheepdog's night-time activities. "I wonder where she's gone."

The children were still crying.

Eventually, just south of Glastonbury, a small black lump was spotted near a hedge. Initially, they thought it was a discarded bin bag. But when the bin bag caught a whiff of sausages and raised its head, revealing pointy ears and a curious nose, they knew it was Margot.

"Stay there, I'll get her!" said the farmer, parking the truck and leaping over a five-bar gate.

The children bounced up and down excitedly on the back seat, clapping their hands and squealing. Now they were crying for joy.

"*Look, Margot, sausages!*" they shrieked. "*We've got sausages!*"

When the farmer reached the curled-up collie, her tail was wagging faintly but she couldn't stand up. She was shivering and exhausted.

"Oh, lass," said the farmer, sweeping her up in his arms. "Whatever happened to you?"

He stroked her soft head and kissed her on the nose, while Margot snuggled under his chin and whimpered. Then he carried her to the muddy pick-up and placed her on a rug on the children's laps.

"Look, here she is," he said.

The children were shocked to see how tired and shabby she looked.

"Don't worry, she'll soon be better," said their mother, patting Margot gently. "A good rest and she'll be right as rain, you'll see."

"She certainly won't be doing any work today, that's for sure," said the farmer.

The late-afternoon drive home was a riot of squirming, licking, shrieking, laughing, wagging and, of course, sausage-guzzling. Margot was feeling better already.

★

Except for an occasional pool of golden light flooding from the streetlamps, the pavements of Glastonbury were dark and abandoned.

"All that glistens is mostings certainly not gold,"[13] muttered the melancholy globbatrotter, dragging the heels of his boots across the concrete slabs.

Nep had never seen the town so quiet – but, there again, he'd never been to Glastonbury at three o'clock in the morning before! He and Merlin trudged along the wide pavements, keeping close to the houses.

"This way," said Nep after an hour's walking. "It'll be safer."

He led Merlin towards the wide-open space of a supermarket car park, away from the houses and streets. Rolling from side to side on his stubby legs, the tired globbatrotter plodded after him, feeling miserable. Although they'd tried to doze for a while under the hedge where Margot had been, they'd been too worried about the missing dog to sleep well.

"'Oh Margot, Margot, wherefore art thou, Margot?'[14]" said Merlin sadly.

"Pull yourself together," whispered Nep.

"I just hopes no one did be stealing her whiles we did be trying to cross that pesky road," muttered Merlin. "After all the bravery she did be summoning on our behalfs, I do be feeling mostings dreadful that we cannot be finding her. I never knew I could be having such heartfelt and deep affections for a dog. It be mostings unusual for a globbatrotter." He hung his head and sighed.

"I'm worried about her too, Merlin, but we've got to keep going. Like she said, we've got to find the antidote. I can't do anything while I'm this small."

"Well, I have been managing, whiles being *this small*, for multitudinous years," grumbled the globbatrotter. "Not all of us can be 'normous, you knows."

"Sorry, Merlin, you know what I mean..."

But the globbatrotter had stopped. His snout was raised, his eyes were closed, as if in a moment of bliss, and his nose was snuffling enthusiastically.

"What is it?" asked Nep.

"Icing buns," smiled Merlin, suddenly energised. "I be sniffing icing buns." He couldn't stop grinning.

"They must have started baking in the shop," said Nep, peering up at the high brick wall at the back of the supermarket. "Come on, Merlin, we can't stop now."

But Merlin had already pushed past him and was scuttling down the path ahead. He'd spotted a partially open door.

"Merlin, no!" hissed Nep, racing after the charging globbatrotter.

But before either of them could reach the door, a hefty dog, attracted by the same appetising smell, trotted round the corner and down the path towards them. On seeing the two tiny creatures, though, the startled dog bounded forwards on stiff legs, barking aggressively.

"Oh great," said Merlin, stopping in his tracks. "Now I do be remembering why globbatrotters be despising dogs. They do be liking to steal all the buns from us!"

Determined not to be stopped in his mission, Merlin growled ferociously at the Staffordshire bull terrier.

"Merlin, don't!" said Nep. "You'll make him angry."

"I be the one who is angry," snarled the globbatrotter.

Nep crouched down, making himself as small as possible, and cowered as the huge Staffie deafened them with his persistent barking. Then, suddenly and quite unexpectedly, Nep could understand what the dog was saying.

"What are you? What are you? You're not usually here!" the dog said. "Go away!"

Nep stood up slowly and shakily, raising his hands above his head. "Look," he said, "I'm a boy. I'm just very small, that's all. Nothing to be frightened of."

On realising that the miniature human could understand what he was saying, and he could understand what the miniature human was saying, the Staffie became even more alarmed.

"Invasion! Invasion! Tiny enemies! Run for your lives!" With his hackles raised, he started to growl.

"It's okay," said Nep, edging forwards. "Don't be scared. I was once big like you, but... but... something happened, you see..."

"Yes, he did be eating too many icing buns," chipped in the globbatrotter, "what did be making him shrink until he was almosts invisible."

"Merlin!" said Neptune, aghast.

The Staffie looked from the tiny boy to the open door and back again.

"No way!" he yelped, then he spun round and shot back up the path.

"Merlin, that was so mean," said Nep.

"No, it was mostings cunning and incredibles clever," said the chuckling globbatrotter, bustling down the path towards the light that shone from the open door. "Icing buns! Icing buns!" he sang to himself.

On reaching his target, Merlin peeped around the door into the brightly lit supermarket kitchen, then his eyes widened and he looked as if he might swoon with delight. A whole crate of freshly baked iced buns had been left on a low shelf to cool, before being put into bags and taken into the supermarket.

"Oh dear," said Nep, seeing them and giving in.

"Goodness graciousness," said Merlin, licking his lips. "I be not able to resists them, Neptune. Let us be grabbing one bun each."

"A whole bun?" whispered Nep. "Merlin, they're bigger than we are! And I don't even like iced buns."

"But they be my mostings favourite," said Merlin, drooling.

CHAPTER 7: SWORD-IN-THE-STONE

"Have you seen what's going on?" said Mei, the vet at the Animal Rescue Centre.

"No, what is it?" said Nadine, putting down her mid-morning cup of coffee.

"There's a swan tapping on the front door. Can you believe it?"

"A swan?" said Nadine in disbelief.

"Yes, and he's very persistent," said Mei. "In fact, I don't know how we're going to get out of this building today."

"That's weird," said Nadine. "There was a swan in a right old flap yesterday, when I rescued the heron."

"Really?"

"Do you think they could be friends?"

"No," laughed the vet. "A swan and a heron? No! Maybe a pair of swans, but not a swan and a heron."

"I'd better come and have a look," said Nadine, getting up. "Stay there, Clive."

Clive, the Labrador, lay down obediently in the staffroom.

When the two women approached the front door, they could see a large male swan pecking at the glass. He looked irritated and upset.

"Well, well!" said Nadine. "He must have followed the car here."

"Don't be silly," said Mei. "Swans don't follow cars – or herons. This must be a coincidence."

"I don't think so," said Nadine, shaking her head. "I really don't think so."

They both stared at the swan, who stopped tapping and stared back at them.

"When can we release the heron?" asked Nadine.

"Very soon," said Mei. "He just needed some warmth, food and rest. He's missing a few feathers, but they should grow back."

"Well, I think we'd better release him today," said Nadine. "And we'd better invite that swan along to the leaving ceremony."

They both laughed.

"I'll go and check on the heron now," said Mei. "If we're not careful, that angry swan's going to break down the door."

★

Merlin belched loudly. Opening his eyes, he rubbed his full tummy and grinned.

"Oh, that were a mostings splendiferous feast. It were a triumph of delectableness."

Nep and Merlin were lying under a bench at the bottom of Tor Hill, surrounded by chunks of iced bun.

"I feel sick," said Nep, wiping his sticky face on his T-shirt. He was surprised at how much he'd been able to eat. Iced buns weren't that bad when you were really hungry.

"Well, I be feeling mostings satisfied," said Merlin contentedly. "Though, methinks, I be not able to be standing up." He tried to force himself into a sitting position, but his round belly was getting in the way.

"Hang on," said Nep, getting to his feet. "I'll help you." He reached out his hand, braced himself and heaved, but he couldn't pull the globbatrotter upright. "No, it's no good," he said. "Try rolling onto your knees, Merlin. See if you can get up that way."

The chortling globbatrotter tried once more to stand up.

"It be not happening," he laughed. "It just be not happening."

Nep scanned the area to make sure no one was about, then he stepped out of their hiding place into the sun. Surveying the expanse of fields, marsh and shining rhynes that made up the Somerset Levels, it looked as though the landscape was spread out before him like an emerald patchwork quilt, with barely a crease in it.

"I can't believe we made it," he said. "It's been quite an adventure."

"This noble journey, it will be recorded by scribes and illustrated by wondrous artists, to be passed down to multitudinous generations what will be following after us," said Merlin. "None of my kind has set trotter in these parts since long before the great flood. It be a marvellous victory, Neptune, and I do be owing it to you."

"Don't be daft," said Nep. "We came all this way together."

With a final push, Merlin was on his feet and admiring the panorama.

"Yeah, but due to your mostings dangerous predicament," he said, "we did venture far beyond Meare. Remember, I be the last surviving globbatrotter in the whole widing world, and you have been bringing I back to the Isle of Avalon – my old ancestral home; the home of Merlin the First. This be truly great."

Nep smiled.

"As the mostings famous bard in the whole of England did say, 'Some are born great, some achieve greatness, and some have greatness thrust upon them.'[15] In this case, greatness, it has been thrust upon you, young sir, but you have been bearing it most nobly."

"I couldn't have reached Tor Hill without you, or Otter, or Swan, or Margot – and Heron, of course."

Merlin's piggy face was crumpling with emotion. "I do hopes they all be safies and soundies. We shall be sharing, for the rest of our days outs and ins, I hopes, the bestest of friendlyships."

"The weird thing is," said Nep, deep in thought, "none of this would have happened if Dad hadn't left home, or if Aunt Morgana hadn't come to stay."

"That aunt of yours, she be a strange one alright."

"Dad said she used to be nice and kind when I was first born, but I've never known her to be like that. As far as I can remember, she's always been rude and stuck-up and mean."

"I do be wondering for how long your Aunt Morgana has been possessed by her evil namesake, the sorceress. I think Morgan le Fay may have been tormenting your aunt for many a year outs and ins. And do be remembering the curse, Neptune; the sorceress could only be appearing once you were raised from a 'babe to a child'. That be when she did start to possess Morgana and regain her power. And soon after, methinks, she did emerge from your aunt to kill your poor, dear mother."

Nep didn't know what to think anymore. It was all so confusing and sad. He turned to face the steep hill.

"It's going to be quite a climb. Do you think you can make it?"

"Of coursings I will be making it," scoffed Merlin. "We globbatrotters are wizards, navigators and renowned explorers. I only be hopings you can be keeping up with I." He set off determinedly up the hill. "I be fuelled on icing buns, remember. There be no stopping I."

★

For three hours, Merlin and Nep searched Tor Hill, climbing higher and higher, as the globbatrotter's nose worked hard to locate the legendary antidote.

"It must be here somewhere," said Nep, scanning the ground. "I'm tired."

"Ah, what be this?" said Merlin suddenly. "Looks! Looks! I knew my hooter could be discovering this mostings magical wort."

Nep dashed over and stood beside him, and together they examined the odd-looking plant that was hidden among tufts of grass, halfway up the hill. Its stem was unnaturally straight. Tiny grey flowers grew on either side of the stem, a bit like a handle on a sword. But, all in all, it was a huge disappointment.

"Is that it?" said Nep. "The special antidote?"

"Yeah, that be it alright."

"But it looks so plain and boring. I don't know how you spotted it, Merlin; it's the most underwhelming thing I've ever seen."

"Well, it be not much to look at, I agree," said Merlin, "but this be possibly the mostings important plant in the whole of Avalon."

Nep didn't look convinced.

"Well, do you want to see if you can be a-pulling it from the ground?" said Merlin. "It must be you what does it, not I. For it is you who does require to be unshrunk."

Nep rubbed his hands together purposefully. Then, bending down, he grasped the stem firmly.

"Oh," he said, "it's cold and hard. It feels like wire – in fact, it's cutting into my skin. I'll never be able to pick this."

"Is you sure you cannot be forcing it out of the earth? We do be needing it mostings urgently."

Nep tried again, but it was like trying to bend iron.

"What are we going to do?" he asked. "We've come all this way and..."

Nep paused. The ground around them was shaking, and he could hear heavy footsteps approaching. Behind them, someone was puffing and panting up the hill.

"Aunt Morgana!" cried Nep, spinning round. "What a surprise! You've... you've woken up! Did you have a nice sleep?"

Nep looked very guilty as he turned to face his irritable aunt who was marching up the steep slope in her smart, heeled shoes. Her frilly collar and neck wobbled with each step. For some reason, she looked even bigger than usual. She was massive.

"Neptune Trout, you are to come with me at once!" she bellowed in her haughty-hippopotamus voice. "I've been searching for you everywhere, you impossible child! Where *have* you been?"

"Um... here. I came out for a bit," said Nep lamely. "With my friend."

Aunt Morgana looked the globbatrotter up and down disdainfully. She didn't seem at all surprised to see him.

"You be knowing who I am, then?" said the globbatrotter suspiciously.

Nep turned to look at Merlin, confused. Then he looked at his aunt. "Aunt Morgana, how do you know Merlin?" he asked.

But then he noticed something odd about her; swirling blue waves of light were shimmering in her green eyes.

"Neptune, darling, aren't you pleased to see me?" smiled his aunt, changing the subject completely.

She never smiles, thought Neptune. *And she never calls me darling.*

"Come on, I've made us some scrummy lunch," she beamed. "You must be starving. Come with me, Neptune. Come on." She held out a plump hand towards him.

"So, is your car here, then?" asked Nep, looking around for her chauffeur and the Bentley. "How did you get here?"

There was no car in sight.

"It's just around the corner," said Aunt Morgana. "Let's go and find it together, darling." She made a grab for Nep's tiny arm, but he dodged out of the way.

"And she be not commenting on your size either," said the wily globbatrotter, scratching his stubbly chin. "When she last did be seeing you, you were much, much bigger, methinks."

"Oh, I was just about to mention that," laughed Aunt Morgana awkwardly. "You do look very funny, I must say!" Nep's aunt had developed a curious, high-pitched cackle. "Look, Neptune, I've got a lovely bedroom ready for you at Wookey Manor. You can come and live with me now. You'll be very happy there, I promise. You'll have everything you could possibly want – and more."

"Won't the clarinet mind?" asked Nep uncertainly.

"The who?"

The whites of her eyes had completely disappeared now; each eye was becoming cloudier and darker by the second, and her face was bulging horribly.

"Oh," said Nep quietly, "it's not you, is it?"

"*Of course, it's me!*" snapped Aunt Morgana, fiddling with her string of pearls. "Come on, Neptune. I can give you a much better life. Your inadequate father will never be wealthy or successful or powerful. You can come and stay with me now. We'll have a lovely time together."

Nep and Merlin started edging backwards up the hill.

"Um... I'm okay, thanks. I think I'll stay here for a bit," said Nep.

"NO, YOU WILL NOT!" shouted Aunt Morgana, losing her temper. Her eyes had become hollow and smoke was wafting from her eye sockets. "YOU WILL NOT STAY HERE! YOU WILL COME WITH ME – IMMEDIATELY!"

"Run!" yelled Merlin.

The two friends dodged around Aunt Morgana's legs and dashed down the slope, but the furious woman raced after them. Then a terrible scream erupted and swirling, angry fog rose into the air. As the body of Nep's aunt collapsed to the ground, dark mist poured out of her eyes and mouth to fill the sky.

Soon Nep and Merlin were surrounded by choking, acrid smoke that halted them in their tracks and turned their blood to ice. Then all the fear drained out of them. They felt cold and listless, unable to move or even care. This was obviously the end of everything.

"I HAVE HAD ENOUGH OF YOU!" screamed the cloud sorceress, her smoky dress writhing above their heads like a tropical storm. "IF I CANNOT HAVE YOU AS MY SON AND HEIR, THEN I WILL KILL YOU! THE CHOICE IS YOURS!"

As they stood beside each other, rigid and enveloped in creeping mist, Nep and Merlin looked pale and broken.

"I'm sorry," whispered Nep to the globbatrotter. "I'm sorry we didn't succeed."

"I be sorry too," replied Merlin. "It has been the mostings honourable honour to be your friend."

Then two things happened at once.

Through the roiling darkness, a large honking swan and a determined heron emerged above Glastonbury Tor, their wings beating fast, their eyes steely. Two sharp beaks ripped into the ominous smog, tearing holes in the cloud sorceress's trailing gown. She had been easy to find; the whole of Glastonbury was obscured by shadow.

"NOT YOU AGAIN!" roared Morgan le Fay, whirling round to swipe at the heron.

At the same time, grassy doorways, like little portholes, burst open all over Tor Hill and small piggy faces peeped out.

"Merlin, is that you?" cried one rosy face with curly hair.

"Aeriene?" whispered Merlin, his voice strangled by the deadly grasp of the sorceress.

"You leave my husband alone!" shouted the irate globbatrotter from her secret doorway. "*Come on, everyone! Get her!*"

Distracted by this new annoyance, the sorceress released her grip on Merlin and Nep, and turned to face the noisy mob.

Globbatrotters appeared all over the hill. Dressed in clothes made out of bin bags and newspaper, with crisp-packet hats and beer-bottle helmets, they charged out of the ground, screaming wildly.

"Look, Merlin!" said Nep, astounded. "Look! Your family!"

But Merlin was completely overcome. His legs buckled and he fell to the ground, weeping.

"*Attack!*" screamed Aeriene, as two smaller globbatrotters rushed after her.

"Edla! Merlin Lefwinus!" sobbed Merlin. "My children!"

A huge battle cry rose up from the globbatrotters as, fearlessly, they rushed towards Morgan le Fay. Some had elastic-band catapults; others carried shields made out of jam-jar lids. And, all the while, rusty-nail swords, kebab-stick spears and small stones were being hurled at the fuming sorceress. As the tiny weapons plunged into her thrashing body, lightning bolts and ear-piercing thunder erupted out of her like a colossal tantrum.

"*Look out!*" yelled Nep, worried for the globbatrotters' safety, as streaks of lightning flashed through the sky and scorched the earth.

"My family," said Merlin, still sitting on the grass, crying. "My long-lost family and friends."

"Yes, and you need to get up and help them!" said Nep, hauling Merlin to his feet.

The globbatrotters retreated a few paces from the deadly storm, while the brave swan and heron banked around the Tor to attack again.

"AAAAAAAAAGGHHH!" ranted Morgan le Fay insanely. "I WILL KILL YOU ALL!"

As Lord Swan and Sir Heron propelled themselves through the sky, the raging sorceress began to spiral – at first slowly and then impossibly quickly. Transforming herself into a lethal cyclone, her whipping winds forced everyone back. As small piggy creatures were flung through the air in every direction, the heron and swan were hurled backwards too, to crash into the Tor and slide to the earth, unconscious. Meanwhile, tiny globbatrotters were blown away like litter in a gale.

"I WILL HAVE NEPTUNE, AND NONE OF YOU WILL STOP ME! HE IS MINE! I HAVE WAITED SO LONG… NOW, GET OUT OF MY WAY!"

The twister gradually stopped spinning and the tempest calmed. The cloud sorceress was reforming in the air. Then she turned her empty, horrible face to stare at Neptune.

"*I hate you, Morgan le Fay!*" shouted Neptune, incensed and defiant. "*You're bitter and evil and cruel. Everyone hates you. Do what you like with me but leave the others alone.*"

"Oh no," murmured Aeriene, picking herself up. "Not the boy."

The heron and swan were still out cold, but the globbatrotters were getting up, dusting themselves down and stepping forward. They were not beaten yet.

Merlin was on his feet too. Finally, he looked resolute and strong.

"I be having just about enough of this vile caper," he said to himself. "We do be needing Arthur Pendragon – and we do be needing him now."

"*It's me you want!*" screamed Nep, hurling his fury at the dark clouds. "*Why don't you just kill me, like my mother? Come on, get it over with! I will never be your son and heir. I don't want to be anything like you. Just kill me now, and let the others live in peace.*"

As Morgan le Fay listened to Nep's words, murderous tentacles of mist crept across the grass towards him. Meanwhile, Merlin the Globbatrotter raised his hands above his head and took a deep breath. It was time for the most difficult and most powerful spell known to his kind. Only the very first Merlin, King Arthur's famous magician, had been able to achieve it. Now he had to say those magical words too – to save the boy and to save them all – but it would be a huge risk.

Powerful words rolled out of him like rumbling thunder:

"I call upon the elements,
the great winds of the world.
I call upon the power of love,
whose name shall be heard.

Strong winds of the south,
cold winds of the north,
summon all your strength;
bring your power forth.

Carry Arthur Pendragon
in tempest and in roar;
hasten him towards us,
and peace and truth restore."

CHAPTER 8: THE MOST PRECIOUS GIFT

As Bob attempted to run down the almost-vertical scree, clouds of dust billowed up behind him. He knew this route was risky, but it was going to be the quickest way off the mountain and down to Namche Bazaar and then Lukla. But the speed of his descent soon got the better of him. As his feet skidded across loose stones, he lost all control and tore down the scarp faster than his legs could carry him.

"Oh no!" he cried, his arms windmilling as he tried desperately to slow himself down.

Rocks and stones rolled down the mountainside with him – in fact, he was in danger of causing an avalanche.

Suddenly, he'd lost his walking pole and was on his back. Next, he felt his rucksack being dragged off his shoulders. Helplessly, he watched it slide away. Then he was plunging down the slope, feet first, going in the wrong direction, heading straight for a large boulder and an overhang. After that, he could see nothing but grey sky.

"Stop, stop, stop!" he shouted in frustration, but there was nothing he could do to slow himself down or avoid the edge of the cliff.

"*Help!*" he screamed as his body scraped along the side of the boulder then left the ground and rocketed through thin air.

Then everything stopped – except for the pounding of his heart and the reeling of his brain. Bob peered around him and whimpered like a child. His fingertips were clinging onto the very edge of the boulder. His feet were swinging back and forth in the breeze. The next ridge below him was a hundred metres away. There was nothing between him and the ground – not even a single tree to cling on to.

"Oh God, I'm going to die," he said. "Oh, Neppy, I'm sorry. I'm so sorry, little guy. I love you so much."

As he glanced around the cliff face below him, he could see no one. Not a single person had witnessed his fall.

Tears streamed down his face now, and he screamed more loudly, "Gwen, I'm sorry! I've let you down. I've let our son down. I'm sorry!"

Then, out of the corner of his eye, he spotted something. To his left, growing out of a tiny crack in the boulder, and just within reach, was a shining plant. Being translucent, its petals were almost invisible, but its green leaves were heart-shaped and beautiful.

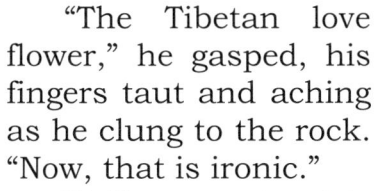

"The Tibetan love flower," he gasped, his fingers taut and aching as he clung to the rock. "Now, that is ironic."

He'd spent his whole life searching for this plant, and now, when he'd finally discovered it, he was about to fall to his death.

Well, what did he have to lose? He only had moments to live anyway. Clutching the rock tightly with his right hand, and frantically trying to find a ledge for his foot to lean on, he reached out and snatched at the little plant with his left hand.

Somehow, he managed to catch hold of two gleaming petals. They looked just like teardrops.

How appropriate, he thought.

One petal slid up his arm and got stuck inside his sleeve, but he put the other one in his mouth. If he was going to die, he might as well experience the power of pure love before he went.

He closed his eyes. This was it. This was the end.

"I love you so much," came a gentle voice in his head. It was Guinevere's voice. "You've been such a great father to our son. Thank you." Her voice was sweet and tender and kind – everything he remembered it to be.

"Oh Gwen," he sobbed.

Bob could feel a soothing presence all around him. It felt as if he was being cocooned in warmth and love – a blanket of angelic protection. A soft light seemed to glow around him and inside him, and he smelt jasmine and honeysuckle in the air.

A sudden realisation hit him. He wasn't separate to the boulder, or the mountain, or the plants, or the birds, or the sky; he was part of it all – an integral part of everything. Time and space meant nothing now. He was part of the universe, and it was part of him. Everything was beautifully connected and intertwined. And the fabric of all creation was love. The threads that held together our cells, our communities, our planets were made of love. Love was the answer to all the world's problems. It was the answer to everything.

As Bob gripped the rock, he understood that life was amazing, and he was privileged to be alive. Life was the biggest prize and the most precious gift that anyone could have. He felt a deep sense of love for every person and every living thing. How sacred it all was.

Then his grip finally gave way and he felt the weight of his body falling through space.

"Help me, Gwen!" he cried.

And, as he fell, Gwen's radiant face was beside him, and her gentle arms were holding him. He was being rocked and comforted, as he plunged down, down, down…

CHAPTER 9: A SPARKLING TEARDROP

A terrifying wind struck Glastonbury that day. The townsfolk had never experienced anything like it. The old Tor rocked from side to side, and people thought it might fall down altogether. The weathervanes on the Church of St John the Baptist were ripped off; two metal cockerels were seen shooting through the sky above the shops and houses, coming to land in the playground of the local primary school.

Everyone ran inside and shut their windows and doors; it wasn't safe to be outside. At the Animal Rescue Centre, Nadine and Mei fastened all the shutters on the windows because the animals were frightened. In fact, it was such unusual weather for August that the storm was mentioned on the national news. No one could ever remember such darkness in summertime.

Above Glastonbury Tor, with no one there to witness it – except for Merlin and Nep, and a host of plucky globbatrotters – a mighty hurricane swept in from the east, carrying with it a man with long shaggy hair and a messy beard. Powerless and fragile in the storm's grasp, Robert Arthur Pendragon Trout had been ripped away from Mount Everest, and the country of Nepal, to be whisked through the heavens at breathtaking speeds. The poor man didn't know if he was dead or alive.

As strange as it may sound, the dangerous gale had actually saved Bob's life. Just before hitting the ground, having fallen one hundred metres from a cliff in the Himalayas, the hurricane had grabbed his helpless body and hurled him westwards around the world, carrying him high above the clouds. Catching glimpses of the Great Pyramids of Egypt, the sapphire blue of the Mediterranean Sea, and just missing the sharp tip of the Eiffel Tower in Paris, Bob thought he was either speeding towards heaven or having some kind of bizarre and shocking dream.

Now, as he approached the Isle of Avalon, a small but powerful globbatrotter – proud descendant of a distinguished wizard – was lowering his hands, allowing the man to sink slowly earthwards, like a flimsy puppet.

"Dad!" screamed Nep, spotting his father floating down from the sky. The boy was engulfed in an eerie mist that threatened to suffocate and destroy him. "Dad, help me!"

As Bob opened his bleary eyes, he found himself hovering, weightless, above Glastonbury Tor. He could hear the tiny voice of his son, but he couldn't see him anywhere. Bob had no idea what had happened or how he'd got here. But the jolt of landing on the tall tower released a single translucent petal from his sleeve, and he watched it flutter downwards, like a sparkling teardrop, into the blackness of a sinister, swirling cloud.

As Bob passed out on the Tor, the menacing shadows dissolved into nothing, the air stilled, the bright sun emerged, and all became quiet.

★

A tsunami of whooping, cheering globbatrotters swept across the grass towards Merlin the Eighth, and lifted him up in an exuberant embrace.

"Merlin!" cried Aeriene, pushing her way to the front of the crowd. "I be thinking you was mostings certainly dead."

"I be thinking the sames about you, my love," cried Merlin, throwing his arms around her robust frame and holding her tight. They rubbed hooters endearingly and gazed into each other's tear-filled eyes.

Then Merlin was hugging and kissing his children, and shaking the hands of the many friendly globbatrotters that surrounded him.

"'Oh wonderful, wonderful, and most wonderful!'" he cried. "'And yet again wonderful, and after that, out of all hooping.'[16] This be the mostings bestest day of my life."

When he remembered himself, Merlin introduced his small friend Neptune to his long-lost family. The clan was about to lead them both into the underground burrows to have the biggest party in globbatrotter history, when Nep explained that he really ought to be growing tall again and rescuing his father from the top of the tower.

"Oh yes," said Merlin, "that be a fair point. There will be plenty of time to be a-celebrating afterwhiles."

Nep took Merlin quietly to one side. "I think I need to do this on my own, Merlin," he said. "It's up to me to work it out, isn't it?"

"Indeedy it is," said Merlin, holding Nep's hands in his meaty fingers. "Very well then. My family and I, we will be awaiting you in the Halls of Avalon, beneath this fine hill. I be wishing you the very bestest of luck, my mostings dearest friend."

Merlin disappeared into the hill with the raucous crowd, and Nep was amazed to see that when the secret doorways were closed, they were completely invisible.

★

Half an hour later, Neptune Trout was sitting staring at the small, sword-like plant. The heron and swan had finally roused and wandered over to see what he was doing. On Nep's right stood the old heron; on his left, the elegant swan. The two birds had aching heads and sore necks, but they stood beside the boy, intent on seeing the quest through to the end.

"It's certainly a puzzle," said Sir Heron.

"Quite so," said Lord Swan. "What are your thoughts, Neptune?"

"I really don't know," said Nep. "I thought that when the storm died down and the sorceress disappeared, this little plant would come out of the soil easily – but I still can't pick it."

The two birds nodded pensively.

Nep continued, "Merlin told me that if this plant could be removed once and for all from the ground, then Morgan le Fay would never be able to come back; it would be the end of her. I just wish I could work out how to do it. If I don't, she might return one day and try to take me away again. She might even try to kill my father. I couldn't bear that."

"It would release the bonds of the whole world, if Morgan le Fay were no longer here to terrorise us," said the heron.

"Sir Heron, we mustn't put any more pressure on the boy," said the swan.

"Wait... what did you say, Sir Heron?" said Neptune.

"I said that this act of removing the sword-in-the-stone, and ending the sorceress's reign of terror, I'm sure it would free us all, not just you."

"Yes, but what were the exact words you used?" said Nep.

"Um... let me think..." said the heron.

"You said it would release the bonds of the whole world," said Lord Swan.

"I wonder..." said Nep. "Maybe that's it!"

"What?" said Heron. "What have I said?"

"There's a spell that Merlin used in the marshes to set us free, when the toads had caught us. The spell untied our ropes and released us. Do you think it could release this plant too?"

"It's certainly worth a try," said Lord Swan. "But won't you need Merlin the Globbatrotter to cast the spell for you?"

"You're probably right," said Nep. "Though I did memorise it."

"Now, now," said the heron to the swan. "Let us see if some of Merlin's creature magick has rubbed off on the boy. After all, Neptune is one of us now – a creature of fur and feather. Give it a try, Neptune. Go on."

"Okay then," said Nep. He stood up and cleared his throat. Then he gripped the plant's hard stem tightly.

Somehow, the words felt right as they flowed from his lips; he understood their power; he believed completely in their magic; he believed in the hope they offered.

> "Good battles evil,
> light destroys the night,
> peace will overcome
> the hate and the fight.
>
> When help is required,
> magick will reply,
> when the foxes bark
> and the owls do cry.

Then bonds will shatter
and all will be free,
as Merlin foretold
at Glastonbury."

Neptune waited, though he wasn't sure what he was waiting for.

"Oh no!" he said. "I've just realised, Merlin said this spell at night-time. There are no foxes or owls around now."

But, as he looked up, to his utter astonishment, several owls were landing on the Tor. He could see a tawny owl, a barn owl and a long-eared owl, among others. They all started hooting loudly – in broad daylight! Then the barking of several foxes could be heard echoing across the fields and town. It seemed as if they all wanted to see the end of Morgan le Fay.

"This certainly is magick," gasped the swan. "The boy is a wizard!"

"Try now," said the heron, nodding at the small plant. "Try now."

Suddenly, the stem felt soft and supple in Nep's hands as he tugged on it. With hardly any effort at all, the sword-in-the-stone slipped out of the ground. And as Nep kept on pulling, roots of two metres in length slithered out of the soil.

"Well, well, well," laughed Sir Heron, his eyes twinkling brightly. "What a remarkable day this is!"

Now all Neptune had to do was chew on the disgusting, foul-tasting root.

"Oh, yuck!" he said, as his face grimaced and he tried not to be sick.

"I think we'll leave that part to you," said Lord Swan.

★

Still retching from eating the horrid root, and trying to come to terms with being so much taller again, Nep watched as Heron and Swan struggled to carry his father down from the high tower. Gripping an arm in each of their beaks, the birds flapped their wings furiously and tried to take Bob's weight. But, despite their best efforts, they all plummeted to the ground, crash-landing in a heap of feathers. At least they'd slowed his descent a little.

"Hey, thank you, dudes," said Bob shakily. "That was like super cool, guys."

Nep ran to his father.

"Dad! Dad!" he yelled, throwing his arms around Bob's hairy neck.

His father held him close, as if he never wanted to let him go ever again.

"Hey, kiddo," smiled Bob. He kissed his son on the forehead, though his eyes were spinning and he still looked dazed.

"Are you okay, Dad?" asked Nep.

"To be honest, son, I'm not really sure what's going on. One minute, I'm in Nepal – in like a really hairy situation, man. The next minute, I'm here in Glastonbury. What's happening, Neppy?"

"It's a long story, Dad, but I'm so glad you're here."

"And what's like happening with all the birds these days? First, some demented goose at Everest Base Camp. Then this crazy swan and heron going like wild, man – like trying to teach me how to fly or something. And all these owls..." he said, peering up.

About twenty owls were taking off from the Tor and flying into the distance.

"Everything's a bit weird right now, Dad. But Merlin the Globbatrotter and I are friends. He travelled here with me."

"Oh, you met old Globby! Sweet, man! He's a great little dude."

"Yes, he hid me in the rhynes, like you asked him to. And he's got a family after all. They live under this hill..."

But Bob was having trouble keeping up.

"Is that your Aunt Morgana down there?" he asked distractedly. "Is she like... okay?"

Aunt Morgana's body was lying on the grass near the bottom of the hill. Flat on her back, she was snoring loudly, her whole body quivering with each breath.

Bob and Nep sprinted down the slope and knelt beside her.

"Morgana?" said Bob, tapping her cheek gently. "Wake up, Morgana." But his sister was comatose.

Then something small and shiny – barely visible – caught Nep's eye. It was lying beside his aunt in the grass.

"What's this, Dad?" said Nep, picking it up carefully with one finger and placing it in his palm. The small petal caught the light and shimmered like a rainbow.

"Oh, like wow, Nep! In the Himalayas, I managed to pick two petals of the Tibetan love flower. That looks like one of them. Wild, man!"

"Dad, you found it!" cried Nep. "It's so beautiful!"

"And it's all true, kiddo. If we had enough petals from that plant, we could save the world: turn hate to love, anger to peace, sadness to happiness. It's so powerful, Neppy. I know because I tried it. I'll never see life in the same way again. It's like... amazingly, wonderfully groovy."

"Dad, I've got an idea," said Nep, holding the translucent petal over his aunt's open mouth.

"Wait!" said Bob. "That's like super valuable, son. It's the only one we have."

"Trust me," said Nep. "I know what I'm doing."

CHAPTER 10: WOOKEY MANOR

"My dearest, darling nephew!" cried Aunt Morgana, hurrying down the steps of Wookey Manor. "How absolutely glorious to see you!" Her voice was joyous and gushing.

She clutched Nep to her ample bosom and held him tight. For a moment, Nep thought he might actually suffocate. A week had gone by, but he still hadn't got used to this new version of his aunt.

"And hello, dearest brother!" she said, kissing Bob many times on his hairy face. "Now, both of you come with me; I've got something to show you."

She took their hands and led them, almost skipping, across the manicured lawns towards the River Axe at the bottom of the extensive gardens.

"I have no idea how you met all these precious little globbatrotters, Neptune, but look, they're having a spiffing time! Theodore has made them some darling little boats and they've been having such high jinks together."

Nep's mouth fell open. About forty globbatrotters, of all shapes and sizes, were sailing on the river. They all stopped to wave at Morgana, Neptune and Bob.

"Well, I couldn't leave them in Glastonbury, could I?" said Aunt Morgana, seeing Nep's shocked face. "They were having to hide away all the time, poor loves. They could only go out after dark because of all the cars and people. They'll be perfectly safe here until their new home is ready for them."

"Their new home?" said Bob, equally surprised.

"Yes, it will be simply wonderful!"

"Where is it?" asked Nep, finally finding his voice.

"Why, the caverns of Wookey Hole, of course. It's all arranged. They'll have lots of room to explore – there are so many caves – and they know they can come and visit us here whenever they like. Once Theodore has made enough little yachts, they'll be able to sail straight to Wookey Manor along the river."

"Thank you, Aunt Morgana," smiled Nep. "You're... you're... so kind."

He still couldn't believe the transformation in his aunt. All it had taken was one little petal. Or was it because he'd removed the sword-in-the-stone plant from the hill? Nep couldn't be sure. But now Aunt Morgana's aim in life seemed to be to spread as much love and cheer as possible. These days, she was a whirlwind of happiness.

"Oh, do let me tell you!" Aunt Morgana beamed. "We had Mistress Otter and her cubs here yesterday for a lovely fish supper. Oh, those cubs are just so cute! And gorgeous! And oodles of fun!"

"And didn't you say the swan and heron dropped by recently, Morgana?" said Bob.

"Yes, yes," she smiled, "they're regular visitors to Wookey – and so polite. Such perfect manners. The only one that isn't invited is your bad-tempered cat Pythagoras," she laughed. "Goodness knows what he'd do to all the little globbatrotters."

"Actually, he's been like pretty mellow since I got back from Nepal," said Bob.

"I've certainly seen him worse," said Nep, raising his eyebrows.

"Oh, and look at what Lord Swan brought us in his beak the other day," cried Aunt Morgana, spinning round like a ballerina. "Such a charming little gift!"

She pointed towards a small ornamental pond. Bobbing along on the water was the Quacking Nancy – and learning to ride on her back were little Edla and Merlin Lefwinus. Their father, Merlin the Eighth, watched proudly from the edge of the pond, shouting instructions in an important voice.

"Hold on tight to those reins now, Edla. That be right, that be right. Well done... Ah, she be a fine vessel, that one," he said. "She be travelling all the way from Meare halfway to Glastonbury. A very fine vessel indeedy." On spotting Nep, the globbatrotter smiled broadly and said, "Hello, small personage... I mean, *large* personage! It be mostings splendiferous to be seeing you again."

Nep, Bob and Morgana watched the boating lesson for a while, then Bob said, "Merlin, there's something I've been meaning to ask you, dude."

"What be that then, Mister Bob?"

"How did that crazy goose on Everest know how to find me, man? Was it like creature magick or something?"

"Oh no," chortled the globbatrotter, "I did be telling all the birds to be searching for the mostings hairy man on the mountain."

Everyone laughed, but they were soon interrupted by the gentle purr of a Bentley on the gravel driveway.

"Oh, here they come!" cried Aunt Morgana, jumping up and down like a schoolgirl. "Our VIP visitors have arrived. They've come for tea – with the dear farmer's permission, of course."

Smiling out of the car's back window, and looking slightly embarrassed, was Margot the sheepdog. She'd been groomed especially for her grand outing; her family had even tied a large bow around her neck. As the chauffeur opened the rear door and bowed, she leapt out and bounded across the grass to meet Nep. And through the open car door, Nep could just make out the other important guest – it was Norman the garden gnome, sitting stiffly on the back seat, wearing a seatbelt. Merlin would be so pleased to see his old friend 'the philosophiser' again.

As an excited Margot jumped up to lick Nep's face, Bob and Aunt Morgana only heard soft whimpers and snuffles, but Nep knew exactly what the collie was saying:

"Oh, how lovely to see you again, Neptune. It really is a pleasure. I can't express how delighted I am to be in your presence once more. And how you've grown! You look so well. Indeed, you do. In fact, I'd go so far as to say, you look exceedingly handsome."

As the clan of globbatrotters strode towards Wookey Manor, to go in for tea, Bob remembered a note he'd picked up in the hallway of their house in Meare.

"I found this letter for you, kiddo," he said to Nep. "I think it's from your friends in the village."

Nep unfolded the note with some trepidation; it was from Mary and Jesh. But, to his great relief, they said they missed him and wanted to see him soon. They hoped they could still be friends.

Nep smiled.

"That's nice. Thanks, Dad. Now I'm big, I'll be able to play with them again."

"What do you mean 'big'?" laughed Bob, completely unaware of his son's antics in the laboratory. "You've still got a fair bit of growing to do, little guy!" Bob patted him fondly on the head.

"Oh yes, you're not very big at all, if you ask me!" said Aunt Morgana, rubbing her fulsome stomach and shrieking with laughter. "Let's go inside and fatten you up, shall we? We've got crumpets, scones, chocolate cake, trifle, shortbread biscuits... oh, and iced buns! Let's not be forgetting the iced buns!"

★

"Merlin?" said Nep.
"Yeah?"
It was late in the evening and Neptune and Merlin the Globbatrotter were lying beside the River Axe, watching the midges dancing over the water in the amber light. They could relax now that the youngest globbatrotters were all tucked up in bed in the many spare bedrooms of Wookey Manor, having been given a bath and read a story by Sir Theodore and Lady Morgana.

"Do you miss the old days?" asked Nep dreamily.

"What, being chased by nasty toads, giant pumas and ferocious storms what do be whirling about mostings menacingly? No, I does not."

"No, I mean you and me," said Nep. "You know, sitting in the Tea & Biscuit, eating plums in Ghost House garden, going exploring together..."

"Oh yeah. Of coursings I be missing that. We did be having some grand old times. But you would be having trouble getting inside the Tea & Biscuit now," he chuckled.

"I know," said Nep sadly. "I miss being small."

"And, in all honestings, Neptune, I do be missing the peace and quiet of my old home," said the globbatrotter. "This be all very grand and mostings pleasant and safe and luxurious an' all, but it not be the Tea & Biscuit – no, it be not."

"Why don't you move in again, then?" said Nep. "I mean, with Aeriene and Edla and Merlin Lefwinus, of course. I could visit you over the garden wall."

"I would be liking that mostings sincerely – though I think I would be needing a bigger teapot," laughed Merlin. "And perhaps some more of Dolly's furniture."

"I'm sure that could be arranged," smiled Nep.

"Anyways, young sir," said Merlin, "don't you still be having some of that old sword-in-the-stone root left?"

"Oh yes, there's loads of it," said Nep.

"And don't you still be having some of your father's Tibetan shrinking toadstools and lamsinpoo in the labor... labora... labora-oratory?"

"Yes?"

"Well then..." said Merlin the Globbatrotter, tapping the side of his orange snout with a chunky finger. "Let us be saying no mores."

THE END

SHAKESPEAREAN REFERENCES

William Shakespeare (sometimes called "the Bard of Avon" or just "the Bard") was born in the year 1564 in Stratford-upon-Avon in England. He was one of eight children to his parents John Shakespeare and Mary Arden. William's father, John, was a maker of gloves. As two of John and Mary's daughters sadly died when they were young, William became the eldest child.

    William married Anne Hathaway when he was eighteen years old, and they had three children together. He moved to London and became a famous poet, playwright and actor. He was a founding member of a group of actors called The Lord Chamberlain's Men.

    For almost 20 years, William wrote two plays every year. He was a very prolific writer! In fact, during his writing career, he wrote 38 plays, 154 sonnets (a sonnet is a poem of 14 lines), 2 long narrative poems, and many other poems.

    Although William Shakespeare lived over 400 years ago, his work is still produced on the stage and screen today, and he is still widely quoted. We get many of our everyday expressions from William Shakespeare, such as:

    A wild goose chase
    A laughing stock
    For goodness' sake
    Neither here nor there
    Eaten out of house and home
    In a pickle
    In stitches
    A heart of gold

> Mum's the word
> Vanish into thin air
> A sorry sight
> Full circle
> All of a sudden
> Knock knock! Who's there?

William Shakespeare is one of the most important writers in English history. He died in the year 1616.

As you will have noticed, in the novel *The Globbatrotter*, Merlin the Globbatrotter admires William Shakespeare (or "the Bard") greatly. However, although the globbatrotter loves Shakespeare's writing, he sometimes gets it wrong! These are the Shakespearean quotations that are mentioned in the story, as they should be written:

1. Shakespeare's real words were, "To be, or not to be, that is the question." Prince Hamlet says these words in the play *Hamlet*.

2. The full quotation, from the play *The Tempest*, is: "We are such stuff as dreams are made on, and our little life is rounded with a sleep."

3. The correct quotation, from the play *Julius Caesar*, is: "Cry 'Havoc!' and let slip the dogs of war." These words are spoken by the character Marc Antony.

4. When the globbatrotter talks about the "green-eyed monster" (referring to the evil toad), he has misunderstood Shakespeare's words in the play *Othello*. Shakespeare actually writes: "O beware, my lord, of jealousy; it is the green-eyed monster…"

Therefore, Shakespeare thinks that being jealous or envious can make us monstrous.

5. The correct quotation is: "Friends, Romans, countrymen, lend me your ears." (This has nothing to do with Norman!) Again, these words come from the play *Julius Caesar*, and they are spoken by the character Marc Antony.

6. The full quotation, "Good night, good night! Parting is such sweet sorrow, that I shall say good night till it be morrow" is said by Juliet in the play *Romeo and Juliet*.

7. The quotation "Thank me no thankings, nor proud me no prouds" also comes from the play *Romeo and Juliet*.

8. "He has not so much brain as ear-wax" – this is said in Shakespeare's play *Troilus and Cressida*.

9. "Once more unto the breach, dear friends" is the correct quotation from the play *Henry V* (a "breach" refers to a gap in the walls of Harfleur). King Henry V says these words during the siege of Harfleur in Normandy in 1415. He is basically saying to his troops, "Let us try to attack again."

10. In Shakespeare's play *Coriolanus*, the actual words are: "Hence rotten thing! Or I shall shake thy bones out of thy garments."

11. "The course of true love never did run smooth" is a quotation from the play *A Midsummer Night's Dream*, and these words are spoken by the character Lysander.

12. "We have seen better days" is quoted correctly by Merlin the Globbatrotter. These words come from the play *Timon of Athens*, and are said by the character Flavius. But William Shakespeare liked this expression and used it in several plays, including *As You Like It*.

13. "All that glisters is not gold" (note that Shakespeare says "glisters" and not "glistens") are words from the play *The Merchant of Venice,* said by the Prince of Morocco.

14. In the following quotation, Juliet is calling for Romeo (not Margot!) in the play *Romeo and Juliet*: "O Romeo, Romeo, wherefore art thou Romeo?"

15. In the play *Twelfth Night*, the full quotation is: "Be not afraid of greatness. Some are born great, some achieve greatness, and some have greatness thrust upon them."

16. "O wonderful, wonderful, and most wonderful! And yet again wonderful, and after that, out of all hooping" is a quotation from the play *As You Like It*.

ACKNOWLEDGEMENTS

I'd like to thank my family – Andrew, Will and Ana – for their wholehearted support while I've been writing this novel. I started writing this story many years ago, and it was through your encouragement and enthusiasm, Will and Ana, that I picked it up and began again. Andrew and Ana, thank you for reading a couple of drafts of this novel and for always responding positively and urging me to continue. Thank you also to my mum, Gill Groark, for your constant belief in me.

I'd particularly like to thank Dewin Blewog for his brilliant illustrations. He's really captured the essence of the story and portrayed the characters and scenes with such understanding and creativity. Liaising with him while writing this story has brought me much joy. *Diolch yn fawr* / thanks a lot!

Thank you to my mother-in-law Prue and my late father-in-law James for many enjoyable tours of the Somerset Levels over the years. You've inspired me to love this unique landscape and the town of Glastonbury. Thank you for your kindness and for the many happy memories.

My brother Jim Groark, an experienced mountaineer, has been a mine of information about climbing, the country of Nepal, and the route to Everest Base Camp. Thank you, Jim, for your wonderful support and knowledge, and for answering my many, many questions!

Huge thanks to my cousin Susan Davies and her reading-group friends Susie Mortimore and Marisa Waymouth for taking the time to read this novel and for offering such valuable feedback and encouragement. I'm also grateful to a few younger readers, including Owen and Ethan Mould, and Mrs Janet Hughes' pupils, for reading my manuscript and responding so enthusiastically. Thank you, Janet, for including some chapters of this novel in your busy teaching schedule.

Last but not least, heartfelt thanks to Kelli Hill of Ginger Fyre Press for your eagle-eyed attention to detail, and to Diane Narraway and Marisha Kiddle for publishing this novel. Your faith in my writing has cheered me on.